MW00681437

Carrying a Load of Feathers

by

Bill McBride

First Edition

Copyright 2009 by Bill McBride
ISBN: 978-0-692-00099-1

To Order more copies, go to:
www.underoneroof.org
or call 1-415-503-2300

Under One Roof is a charity in San Francisco. Half the proceeds of each sale go to this charity.

For information on the Author's Workshops, go to:
www.entertaininganelephant.com

Dedication

To those who have chosen
to teach love rather than fear.

Bill McBride

More Titles by Bill McBride

Entertaining an Elephant, © 1997,
Order at www.underoneroof.org.

Building Literacy in Social Studies, © 2007,
Order at www.ascd.org.

If They Can Argue Well, They Can Write Well, © 2008,
Order at www.incentivepublications.com.

Acknowledgments

A Course of Miracles
Copyright 1975, 1985 Foundation of Inner Peace,
PO Box 598, Mill Valley, CA 94942
Reprinted with permission.

"Autobiography in Five Chapters" from There's a Hole in My Sidewalk: The Romance of Self-Discovery by Portia Nelson. Copyright 1994. Beyond Words Publishing, Hillsboro, Oregon. Reprinted with permission.

Illusions: The Adventures of a Reluctant Messiah by Richard Bach. Copyright 1977 by Richard Bach and Leslie Parrish-Bach. Published by Dell Publishing Co. Inc., a division of Random House, Inc. New York, NY 10017. Reprinted with permission.

Making a Life, Making a Living by Mark Albion Copyright 2000 by Mark Albion and Wordworks, Inc. Published by Warner Books, Inc. 1271 Avenue of the Americas, New York, NY 10020

"On Crime and Punishment," *from The Prophet* by Kahlil Gibran. Copyright 1923 by Kahlil Gibran and renewed 1951 by Administrators C.T.A. of Kahlil Gibran Estate and Mary G. Gibran. Alfred A. Knopf, a Division of Random House, Inc. New York, New York, 10019 Reprinted with permission.

Selections from Early Greek Philosophy by Milton C. Hahm. Copyright 1964 by Appleton-Century-Crofts 440 Park Avenue South, New York, NY 10016

"A society grows great when old men plant trees under whose shade they know they shall never sit."

Greek Proverb

Musical Accompaniments

From the author:

     As I wrote this book, I often listened to my favorite songs on my iPod. It occurred to me that a number of these songs reflected the feelings and beliefs of specific characters in each chapter. I decided to add a musical dimension to the book by providing those songs and the artists performing them.

     Below are the songs I attached to each chapter. You might want to download them into your MP3 player and create a Playlist so you can play each song as you finish a chapter. I hope you enjoy them.

Chapter 1: "A Case of You" sung by K. D. Lang

Chapter 2: "Down to Zero" sung by Joan Armatrading

Chapter 3: "Stuck in a Moment" sung by U2

Chapter 4: "Sitting" sung by Cat Stevens

Chapter 5: "Superman" sung by Five For Fighting

Chapter 6: "Let's Get It Started" sung by Black Eyed Peas

Chapter 7: "Everybody Is A Star" sung by Sly and the Family Stone

Chapter 8: "Follow Me" sung by Peter, Paul and Mary

Chapter 9: "Never Comes the Day" sung by The Moody Blues

Chapter 10: "Cat's in the Cradle" sung by Harry Chapin

Chapter 11: "Rhymes and Reasons" sung by John Denver

Chapter 1

Week One, Day One

The black Platinum Edition Cadillac Escalade swung abruptly into the center lane, cutting off a bright red Mini-Cooper. The driver of the Escalade looked in his rear-view mirror when he heard a muffled beep from behind. He could just make out the white roof of a small car.

"What's your problem? You shouldn't be driving a soup can anyway," he hollered at the driver of the Mini.

The phone on the dash rang.

"Hello. This is Bradford."

"Bradford, it's Jason."

"What's up man? You making me some money today?"

"Looking good, Bradford. I spent the day with the three salesmen over in the valley. Most are doing good."

"Any not hitting their numbers?"

"Jackson is down about forty percent."

Bradford saw red brake lights begin to cascade down the highway towards him.

"Damn!"

"It's not that bad, Bradford. I think we can get him up to his quota."

"I suggest you do, Jason. A five-year old could get people to sign on the dotted line in this market. We're expecting you to go over your number, you know."

"I know. I know. Don't get riled. I'll ride his butt hard this week."

"Good, cause I'll be riding yours. Remember, you don't make your bonus, then I don't make mine, and then I'm not very happy. Anything else?"

"No. Just wanted to update you."

Bradford hung up on him. Glancing to his right, an attractive woman pulled up beside him in a silver mini-van. He accelerated to match her speed until he saw her yelling at kids strapped in the back seat.

Up the freeway, traffic was beginning to back up again. Suddenly the woman pulled ahead and darted right in front of him. He hit the brakes, feeling the shoulder strap pull against his new suit.

"Damn!" he yelled, slamming his fist against the horn and holding it there. "You idiot!"

He looked quickly over his left shoulder into the next lane. The red Mini-Cooper was pulling up. He shoved his right foot against the gas, felt the eight cylinders kick in and swung the wheel left. A familiar beep sounded behind him as he pulled into the left lane and alongside the van that had just cut him off. He glared at the woman but she was oblivious, still screaming at the crying kids in the back.

Turning his eyes back up the road, he spotted his exit only thirty yards ahead.

"How the hell did I end up in the center lane?" he mumbled. Seeing an opening in front of the van, he hit the gas and swung the Escalade back to the right, causing the lady in the van to hit her brakes. The black behemoth sailed across her path and up the right exit ramp.

"Payback, missy," he yelled in his rear-view mirror. His heart racing, Bradford turned into the road leading to his housing development. The security guard saw him coming and spun in the gatehouse for the lift button.

"Hello, Mr. Sparks," called the uniformed man as the car sailed past. Mr. Sparks stared straight ahead.

Bradford had moved his family into this new development a couple of years ago when it opened, after he was promoted to regional manager. It still annoyed him that the homes loomed so unnaturally large on their landscaped lots. This land was once prairie so the newly planted trees were mere twigs beside the five bedroom, five bath homes. McMansions some called them.

He grinned when his home came into view, or should he say his tree. In this flat pasture turned development, one large tree remained. Bradford was sure that grazing cows once sought its shadows in the noonday heat. The developer must have known that, like a corner lot, the tree would increase a property's value. Bradford had gotten into a bidding war over this tree, running up the price of his lot by seven thousand dollars, but he won. The tree now shaded most of his backyard. You don't beat Bradford, he reminded himself.

As he swung the Escalade into his driveway, he skidded to a halt in the gravel. A cloud of dust flowed past the Escalade. His daughter's Honda was parked in *his* parking space.

"I'll kill her," he mumbled. "I have been very clear with them on this."

The house had a three-car garage. The first was Bradford's; the second was for Allison's gold Lexus. Kelley's Honda got the third spot, and his son parked his used Ford Focus on any space left.

He pulled the Escalade within six inches of the rear of her car, then placed his hand on the horn and pressed, holding it there.

Kelley was in the kitchen talking to Maria when she heard the horn.

"Oh hell," she cried.

Maria's eyes grew wide. Both knew that horn.

"I can't believe he's home so soon. I'm dead!"

She grabbed her keys and bolted out the garage door. She ran past her car and up to her dad's window.

"Dad, I'm sorry. I just ran in for a . . ."

"Kelley!" he screamed over the horn, staring straight ahead. "Move the damn car!"

Kelley stared into the tinted glass for a second, then ran past the deafening horn to her car. Her hands were trembling as she turned the keys in her hand, and she dropped them. Reaching down in the gravel, she touched the car alarm as she picked them up.

The Honda screamed in response, lights flashing. As she pushed the alarm button she glanced back at her father; his forehead was resting on the steering wheel. His hand was still firmly planted on the horn.

Kelley jumped in the car, wiped her eyes, started the car and put it in reverse. She looked back, waiting for her dad to back up so that she could move, then realized he wouldn't. The gravel crunched as she edged forward, then backward. Forward, then backward. Forward, then backward. Forward, then backward. And finally, on the last forward she squeezed out of the tight spot and pulled over to her proper parking spot.

Kelley sat motionless, taking short quick breaths. She heard the horn stop, the Escalade door slam, the gravel crunch under her father's Italian shoes, and the garage door into the house slam shut. She lowered her head to the steering wheel, feeling wet drops splatter on her bare legs. She was not about to go inside crying.

She took a few deep breaths, then yelled "Jesus" when thumps hit her side window.

She turned to see a blue and gold football jersey.

"Nope, I'm not the Messiah, so you're still in deep kimchi," replied a deep voice.

"Go away."

"Come on, Kelley Kookoo. What's up?"

"Go away, Christopher," she called, resting her head back on the steering wheel.

"Hey, now that the air raid is over, I thought you might want to come out of the shelter."

Kelley smiled.

"Are you sure there aren't any cluster bombs out there?" she called from inside the car.

"They're everywhere. You know Bradford."

Another tap on the window. Kelley wiped her eyes, reached for the door handle and climbed out into the open arms of her brother.

*   *   *   *   *

Maria opened the door of the stainless steel professional grade Viking oven and peered inside. A deep aroma of sizzling beef flooded the room. Everything looked okay. It should be medium rare shortly.

As she closed the oven door, she heard the garage one open. Without turning around she said, "Any survivors out there?"

"Where is he?" responded Christopher. Maria turned to face him. God how he had grown, she thought. When she first took the job as these kids' nanny, they were still babies. Kelley was four and Christopher two. Now Kelley was a young lady, a senior in high school. Looking like a Midwestern farm girl, she had her mother's auburn hair, green eyes and freckles. Like all her friends, she was always watching her weight.

Chris on the other hand had picked up the genes of the patriarch of the family. Only a sophomore, he was already 6'1", as tall as his father and with shoulders just as broad. His face was still boyish though, perhaps because of the blond hair and blue eyes, but he was handsome.

"My how these pretty people breed," thought Maria.

"Your father went back to his study," she replied. "He said not to disturb him."

"Is mother around?" asked Kelley as she reached for the oven door. Maria slapped her hand before it made contact.

"Don't be messing with my beef," she said in mock sternness. "Your mother went to the spa. She came back a while ago and took a nap. Now she's having her 'attitude adjustment'."

"Wow, must have been a hard day at the spa?" quipped Chris.

Maria grinned and began pouring the steamed rice from the stainless pot into a casserole. She sprinkled fresh Italian parsley on top.

"Now don't be catty young man. She had to interview gardeners all morning."

"Gardeners?" asked Kelley as she reached into the large salad bowl for a carrot. Her hand never made it.

"Girl, get out of my greens!" said Maria swinging.

In twelve years Kelley had never gotten her hand out of the way in time. Maria had the peripheral vision of a rabbit and the strike of a rattlesnake.

"We already have a gardener. Why do we need a new one?" asked Kelley, rubbing the top of her reddening hand.

"Well, you HAD one gardener, now you got a new one. Your mother has decided that we will win the

Farmington Fall Landscape Trophy. She said she wants to redo the back yard. She's hired somebody, and he'll be staying in the downstairs apartment of the guest cottage in the back."

Chris pulled up a bar stool to the pass-through counter. He banged the salt and pepper shakers together repeatedly.

"Does dad know?" he asked.

Maria reached for a serrated knife and began slicing through a loaf of French bread.

"I imagine he will know soon enough."

Chris and Kelley caught each other's eyes.

"Here we go," said Kelley.

Maria scooped up the sliced bread and dumped it into a basket. She handed it to Kelley.

"Okay, Chris. Dinner is ready. Go get your parents. Kelley, help me set the dining room table."

Kelley took the bread into the dining room and set it by the silver butter dish. In the pantry she retrieved the silk placemats and silverware. Maria had already set the every day Sasaki dishes at the end of the eight foot mahogany table. Kelley placed the napkins and the utensils down precisely as she had been taught. The silver glimmered under the lights of the crystal chandelier.

Chris strode down the long hallway to the back of the house and found his mom where he knew she'd be, sitting on the sun porch that overlooked the backyard, martini in hand. From the flush on her face Chris guessed it was her second.

"Mom, Maria says dinner is ready."

Allison turned her head slowly towards her son.

"Ahh, I see. It's pot roast Monday. How exciting," she sneered.

Chris stood silently, hoping she would move. Allison reached into the martini, fished for the olive, plucked it into her mouth and smacked her lips.

"Chris, be a dear and make your mom one of your good martinis. Nice and dry. I'll need it to get through the meal."

Chris's shoulders slumped but he knew better than to argue.

"Okay, but come on. Maria says it's ready."

Allison waved him away with the back of her hand.

Before making the drink, he decided to get his dad first. He continued to the room at the end of the first level, pausing at the closed door, leaning in to listen. He could hear his dad on the phone, yelling. Not a good time, he thought. Falling back against the wall, he let his weight slowly pull him to the carpet, waiting for the voice inside to cease. He buried his head between his knees. A moment later--silence. He waited. Nothing. Okay, now! He jumped to his feet and knocked.

"Dad, Maria said it's dinner."

"Damn!" came his father's voice. "All right. I'm coming. Get your mother."

Bradford demanded that the family have dinner together any night that he was not away on business. Why? wondered Chris. Is he a glutton for punishment?

Maria had sliced the roast. She scanned the table for any missing items. Oops, no horseradish. She scurried to the refrigerator, dumped a jar of horse radish into a bowl, threw in a teaspoon, ran it into the dining room and placed it by Bradford's plate. One last look and she headed to the kitchen, squeezing past Kelley as she took her seat on one long side of the table. Untying her apron, Maria hung it in kitchen the pantry, then walked deliberately to her room in the back of the house to watch her evening news.

Kelley sat alone, listening, waiting. She could hear Chris shaking the martini container in the den. A few minutes passed, then he walked in and took his seat opposite her.

"Is she coming?" asked Kelley softly.

"Who knows," Chris responded, shaking his head.

"What's for dinner? It smells wonderful!" Bradford chimed as he strode into the dining room.

Kelley and Chris rolled their eyes at each other.

"It's Monday, dad." said Kelley.

Bradford sat, put the napkin in his lap, then stared down at the empty seat at the end of the table.

"Where's your mother?"

Neither Chris nor Kelley offered an answer.

"Damn it to hell!"

"I'll get her," said Chris starting to rise.

"No!" called out Bradford. "You already screwed that up once. Sit!"

Bradford rose quickly, throwing his napkin into his plate. He strode out of the room.

"Here we go," said Chris, looking down at his empty plate.

"Hey," said Kelley, kicking him under the table. "It's pot roast! Yum! Eat."

Chris took his fork and speared two large chunks of beef. He looked up at Kelley who sat motionless.

"Eat up, girl. It's Maria good!"

Kelley scrunched up her face as if nauseous. She saw a chance to escape any more drama.

"Nah, I'm not hungry, got a lot of homework to do."

She pushed back from the table and headed upstairs. Chris stared at the empty chairs, then filled his plate with beef and bread and took it upstairs to his room.

*   *   *   *   *

Bradford found Allison slumped in her wicker chair, staring out at the backyard.

"What do you think of a Japanese Zen garden?" she slurred when she heard him enter.

"Why aren't you at the table?" he demanded.

"I'm ruminating. I'm envisioning. I'm visualizing."

"Allison, what the hell are you talking about?" He moved in front of her, blocking her view.

"We need peace, Bradford. And as a trophy wife, I need a trophy. I'm determined to win the Farmington Fall Garden Trophy this year. So our new gardener is going to put in a Japanese Zen garden. "

Bradford looked over his shoulder into the backyard.

"What new gardener? Have you hired someone without talking to me first? We HAVE a gardener."

"Had, Bradford. H – A – D, had. And what we had was an illegal alien who mowed the lawn for the pittance you paid him. I'm just protecting you dear. You know how the police are cracking down on all those slaughter houses in the Midwest and poultry plants in the South. The ICE police could raid us at any moment. Your company wouldn't like that, would they dear? Plus, we only have two weeks to redo the entire backyard so I needed a professional," she said, raising her eyes to meet him and showing a faint smile.

"Damn you, Allison. Two weeks? How much will this cost? Do you purposely try to irritate me?" he hissed. His face had grown red with rage.

"Yes" she responded dryly.

Allison reached for her martini, but Bradford grabbed her wrist and twisted it.

"Listen here. You'll not go over my head, do you hear me? Now get your butt to the dinner table and at least act like a mother eating with her children."

He threw her hand back at her face, turned and hit the sun porch door with his fist as he exited outside. Bradford spotted the man in the back left corner of the yard. He wanted to deal with this immediately. As he strode across the lawn, he reached into his right pocket for a twenty to pay him off.

Allison watched him walk in his "I'm-gonna-kick-your-butt" stride. Imagine, she had once found him titillating. She picked up her martini and snuggled back down into her chair, smiling. Her wrist stung and showed his finger marks.

"Hey! Hey, you!"

The short man in the corner didn't turn around.

"Oh, great," he thought. "She's hired a deaf mute."

Bradford walked up beside the man. He was dressed in old khakis, a red and grey plaid shirt, and scuffed tan work boots. He wore a floppy hat.

"Hey, *hable Ingles*?"

The man turned to face him. He had deep brown eyes, each lit with a small sparkle.

"Yes sir, I do. And I need to let you know that we'll need to begin by getting rid of all this oxalis."

"The what?" asked Bradford. "No, look, my wife has made a . . ."

19

"This oxalis, sir, will spread throughout your yard. It sends long tentacles underneath the soil and comes up everywhere. As you can see clearly in this area, it is already spreading like a virus."

"What? What are you talking about." asked Bradford, suddenly concerned about an alien life form that was infecting his yard.

The gardener squatted down and pointed to a small three-leaf plant. He motioned for Bradford to join him. Bradford looked back over his shoulder at the sun room, then tugged his trousers up and squatted down.

"That?" said Bradford. "That's nothing but clover."

"Well, as they say sir, things are often not what they appear. This is actually oxalis."

Bradford squatted down and pulled up the plant.

"There," he said. "Job's done."

The man pointed to another. Bradford yanked it out. The man pointed to another. Bradford yanked it out too. The man pointed to another.

Bradford reached, then stopped. He suddenly felt exhausted, beaten. Just too many anxieties today, too many.

The man picked up one of Bradford's remnants.

"I'm afraid, sir, that if you don't pull up the roots also, the oxalis simply continues to spread."

"How much is she paying you?" he sighed.

"She said that was your decision," he responded, then pointed to another clover.

"Well, I can't see paying much for someone to pull weeds."

"Then sir, might I suggest you cover my room, board, and gardening expenses, and then you can pay me whatever you think I'm worth when the job is done."

Bradford's eyes lit up.

"Sounds reasonable to me. So when is this garden competition?"

"It is two Saturdays from now, sir."

"She's got you living in the coach house?"

"Yes sir."

"Well, if the competition is on a Saturday, then you should be finished on the Friday before. You'll get a check under your door that night. That's your exit, understand?" Bradford said, yanking at another piece of clover.

The gardener reached down and pulled the remainder of the stem out of the ground. "Yes, sir."

Bradford gave the gardener a suspicious look. "Hey, you got any references for grass pulling?"

The little man cocked his head sideways, then smiled.

"Why yes, I refer to Walt Whitman from *Leaves of Grass* who said 'This is the grass that grows wherever the land is and the water is. This is the common air that bathes the globe. This is the breath of law and songs and behavior. This is the tasteless water of souls...this is the true sustenance."

Bradford stared at him wide-eyed. He stood up, looking down at the man. A Mexican probably. Short and brown.

"Just clean the crap out, will ya?" he said, turning back towards the house.

"Yes sir." replied the gardener. "That is my intention."

Music: "A Case of You" sung by K. D. Lang.
For Chris and Bradford

Chapter 2

Week One, Day Two

*Many do not think about the things they experience,
nor do they know the things they learn;
but they think they do.*

--Heraclitus

Coach Walker lifted his right leg, then slammed his steel-toed boot into the right shoulder pad of the left tackle. The boy went sprawling onto the ground, knocking over the guard.

"What did I tell you about being in a solid three-point stance, boy? Huh?"

He spit out a long stream of brown tobacco juice. Most landed in the grass in front of the boy's face mask, but some sprayed onto his helmet. The boy started to jump up, but Walker kicked him down again. This time he placed his foot on the side of the boy's helmet, pressing down with his weight.

"When you gonna' learn? If I can knock you over with one kick, your opponent is gonna' kick your ass. All right, everybody on the line, ten pushups! If I can knock over one more of you wimps, then it's three laps."

Among muffled curses, the boys stretched into the pushup position as Walker called out the numbers.

Chris watched the scene in dismay. He was glad Coach Preston took the backs. Preston was tough, but he was a decent man. If he knocked you down, he picked you back up.

"Sparks!" yelled Coach Preston. "What you day-dreaming about? You're up. You better get your mind in the game, kid! Let's go. Run 17 long!"

Chris moved up under the center. He checked his ends. Both were lined up correctly.

"42 – 20 – 17, Hut, Hut!"

The football slapped into his palms. He back-pedaled, then looked once to the right to draw off the defense. By this time, he knew where Tim should be, streaking down the left sideline. He turned and threw. The ball sailed far over Tim's head.

"Great throw there, Sparks," called out Coach Preston. "I see you're still trying to take McDaniel's job."

With head bowed, Chris took his place in line behind the other two quarterbacks. I suck, he thought. Then he felt an arm around his shoulder. He knew that arm. It was Chase McDaniel, the senior quarterback.

"Hey stupid. How many times you gonna' make the same mistake?"

Chris looked up at Chase. "Which one this time?"

"Uh, that would be the one where you don't plant your back foot before you throw. Jeez man, get in the game!"

Chris cringed. Criticism was standard on the football field, but from Chase it stung doubly. Chase wasn't just any senior; he was first string. In fact he was first string at everything—sports, looks, partying, and most especially, girls. He hooked up most anytime he wanted and bragged with teammates about his exploits with different girls. Most everything Chris had learned about sex came from Chase's stories.

Chase had taken Chris under his wing for some reason since the beginning of the season, giving him pointers, working on his timing, telling him which

23

defensive back would try to take his head off. Chris listened to the older boy intently. He studied his every move on and off the field. How he threw a pass to an end or to some hot babe. He was so frigging cool. Why couldn't he be like Chase?

Preston blew his whistle. "Okay, we do five speed drills. Last in each group does a lap. Rest of you get to the showers."

Chris might not throw well but he could run. He regularly beat the other backs in sprints, even Chase. The coaches tried once to make him a defensive end, but he lacked the coordination to react quickly to an opponent.

After sprints, the team crowded into the steamy locker room. Chase was holding court as usual. The juniors and seniors were given their own sections of lockers by the showers and mirrors. Underclassmen were farther away and by the entrance where everyone tracked in the dirt from the playing field. The guys were in different stages of pulling off their practice uniforms. The tile floor was covered in clay from the boys' cleats, and the air was saturated with the acidic smell of sweat.

"All right men, we need to rap tonight!" called Chase to the other upperclassmen. A loud cheer filled the room. Chris looked up and caught the same scared look in every other underclassman's eye. A "rap" was really a "call and response." It was a Freeman High School tradition. The team Captain yelled out either a cheer for an individual Freeman player or an insult to an opposing team or a Freeman underclassman. The players responded. Chase started clapping out a rhythm; the upperclassmen joined in.

"Uh huh, uh huh, who is the best?" sang Chase while gyrating his hips.

"Freeman, Freeman is the best," responded the upperclassmen.

"Uh huh, uh huh, who's the best right tackle?" sang Chase.

"Payton, Payton, is the best right tackle," responded the team, pointing to Levon Payton as he bowed to his teammates.

"Uh huh, uh huh, who's the best defensive back?" sang Chase.

"Killer, Killer is the best defensive back," sang the team as they pointed to Antonio Johnson who raised his hands, palms upward as if to say, "Who else?"

This continued for a while as Chase wound his way through the team. During the show, the underclassmen hurriedly changed into their clothes, most not showering. Chase began to move over to the other end of the locker room. The upperclassmen followed. Phillips in the back had just taken off his jock and twirled it over his head to get Chase's attention.

"Uh huh, uh huh, who's the worse receiver?" sang Chase.

Now everyone knew. The dye had been cast.

"Uh huh, uh huh, Carlson is the worse receiver."

Chris knew all of this was orchestrated down on the field beforehand. The hazing took place at least twice a week. Steve Carlson was standing in his boxers when he heard his name called out. He was what the coaches secretly called a PD—practice dummy. Freeman was a small school so underclassmen were put on the varsity team in order for the first string to have someone to practice against. Steve was a skinny kid weighing no more than 130 pounds. Because he wore glasses, his helmet had a plastic shield to protect his eyes, but it also made it difficult for him to see the football descending through the stadium lights. Not a good handicap for someone who wanted to be an end; hence, he had been dubbed "Can't Catch It Carlson." Every underclassman looked right at him when they heard his name, then backed away. He reached for his gym bag but a hand caught his wrist.

"No! Come on guys, don't!" he pleaded.

The larger boys grabbed his arms. Steve struggled but could not free himself. Phillips came up from behind, turned the moist jock strap upside down so that if would fit snugly, then pulled it over Steve's face so that the wide part wrapped around his chin and the narrow part fit over his nose. Groans erupted from the younger players. Steve gasped for breath, horrified. Phillips tied the jock securely onto his head. Then the boys picked him up and carried him out of the locker room. Chris and the other boys followed. It was understood that all would participate.

Steve jerked his head left and right, trying to throw off the rancid jock strap. He kicked into the air but the players grabbed his legs, holding him high above them. He heard the gym doors being kicked open and then the sudden loudness of girls' voices chanting in unison. The Varsity Cheerleaders!

The girls burst into laughter as the team carried the skinny boy with the jock strap on his head into the middle of the gym, then set him down on the wooden floor. Steve instantly jumped up and ran back for the locker room, but Dawson tripped him up. He skidded across the gym floor on his stomach, causing his boxers to come halfway down. Chase walked over and pulled his boxers down to his ankles.

Squeals of laughter erupted from the girls and players. Another player ran up and started taking pictures with his cell phone. The boy grasped frantically at his underwear with his right hand while trying to cover his privates with his left. His underwear ripped at the waistband as he pulled. Steve scrambled up and bolted into the locker room. The upperclassmen laughed hysterically, slapping high fives, then ran after Steve into the locker room. They surrounded him at his locker. He faced them, a wild look in his eyes, fists clenched. But rather than another attack, the players started patting him on the shoulders and head, laughing, telling him what a great sport he was. They welcomed him to the team, congratulating him. He was a Freeman player now.

Steve flinched with each pat, smiling weakly. When the players finally left him, he pulled on his jeans and hoodie without showering and headed for the parking lot.

Chris showered, dressed, and hung up his equipment to air out. One thought plagued him throughout. When was his turn to be humiliated and what would they do to him?

He left the locker room and headed for the student parking lot. As he walked down the long sidewalk, he looked ahead at the sea of SUV's and Grand Cherokees, Miatas and Minis, Tundra and Tacoma trucks, even Beamers and Benzes. One would never imagine this was the student parking lot, but this was Farmington. This was new money made in computer technology, pharma research, and real estate.

Chris always parked in the far corner of the lot, embarrassed about his used Ford Focus. He didn't take the chance of parking by someone with a hot car and getting dished. Why couldn't his father give him the things he wanted?

As he wove through the lanes of remaining cars, he passed by a new silver Dodge Ram 4X4 pickup and heard a long moan. He took another step, then decided to check it out. Maybe someone was having sex! Quietly edging back, Chris cautiously looked into the side window. He immediately recognized the hoodie. Crouched in a fetal position across the front seat was Steve Carlson, his face buried in his arms. Chris felt a lump grow in his throat. He lifted his hand to knock on the window, then stopped and hurried away.

*   *   *   *   *

Kelley's cell phone rang as she pulled into the driveway, into *her* parking spot. As she switched off the engine, she looked at the phone. It was Sasha, her best friend. She had known Sasha for five years now, since Kelley's dad had moved them out to the west side, or the "made it" side of town as he called it.

"What's up girl?" asked Kelley, sitting in the quiet car.

"Kel, oh my god, like can you believe how much Turtle gave us to read for A.P. History?"

Turtle was Kelley and Sasha's Advanced Placement History teacher, so called by students because he wore a turtleneck sweater on most days. An older baby boomer teacher with graying hair tied into a ponytail, Turtle entered school everyday carrying a scarred brown leather satchel within which was a grade book, a *New York Times*, and a public library novel, usually about the Civil War or the American Revolution.

"Is it that bad? I haven't looked yet," responded Kelley, eyeing her backpack crammed with heavy textbooks.

"Like yea!" screamed Sasha. "I say we do a split."

"How many pages is it?"

"Like forty! Jesus, does he think it's our only subject?"

"Okay, you take the first twenty, and I'll take the last."

"Cool. What else you got tonight?"

Kelley fiddled with the strap of the backpack until she could open it. Seeing the books would remind her of her homework.

"A little in AP Math. And then something weird for English."

"Like what?" said Sasha.

Kelley could hear a loud whirring sound in the background.

"Where are you?"

"Smoothie Express. Needed a sugar hit before hitting the books."

"You need a sugar hit or a Carlos hit?"

"Can't I have both?" Sasha replied coyly.

"Sugar rush, hell." said Kelley sarcastically. "I know what sugar you're after. Did he even notice you?"

"Uh, yea. But because I changed my order four times, and he got pissed."

Kelley laughed out loud. Sasha had had a crush on Carlos since junior year, but she was invisible to him.

"So, what weird assignment did you get in English?"

"Well, he gave us the 'AP is about depth, not breadth' lecture again yesterday. So today he writes a quote on the board and tells us we have to talk to a family member about it and be ready to read a summary of our discussion in class tomorrow."

Kelley's eyes widened, realizing Sasha would be perfect. She might as well be family.

"Hey, speaking of, you got a minute? Hang on, let me find the ....."

"No way girl. Uh uh. Forgetaboutit."

"Sasha!"

"Nope, why don't you call Travis?"

Kelley pushed her books back into her pack back.

"Why don't you lean over and kiss Carlos?"

Sasha laughed.

"Bye girl. Meet you in the library in the morning to share our splits."

"Bye."

Kelley immediately texted a message to Sasha. "Are you kissing him yet?" Within seconds a "**LOL**" came back. She climbed out of the car and went inside to the kitchen.

Maria was hovering over a flour-covered counter.

"Maria, Maria, Maria, please tell me you're making *empanadas!*" she said coming up behind Maria and wrapping her arms around the short woman.

"Aye. *Mija.* Don't bother me. I'm making the last dough pastries now."

On the white counter were scattered ingredients— flour, salt, olive oil, Pernod and the ice water Maria added to the dough as she mixed it to keep it smooth and firm. Maria had already used the circular cutter to make the six-inch dough pastries, waiting to be filled.

Kelley looked over her shoulder and saw the large cast iron skillet simmering. Leeks, garlic, and *jamón serrano,* or Spanish cured ham, sizzled in olive oil. She reached for a tablespoon and turned towards the skillet, but a stinging slap on her spoon-filled hand stopped her.

"*Mija*, you know better. Now *vamos*. I have to fill these and get them in the oven."

Turning to the oven, Maria picked up the skillet and set it on a hot pad on the counter. From a large bowl, she added chopped eggs and parsley, stirring until well mixed, tasting with a small spoon, and adding dashes of salt and pepper.

Kelley had always loved watching her make the *empanadas*. Every movement was practiced and automatic. She seemed lost in her own world. When she was sure the taste was just right, she began spooning the mixture into each dough circle, making sure not to get it too close to the edges. Once they were filled, she grabbed a small brush, dipped it in the ice water, and moistened the edges of each circle. Then, one by one, she folded over each pastry, crimping the edges to look like a clam shell.

"Maria, can I prick them?" begged Kelley.

Maria smiled, handing her the fork. "Okay, but no fancy stuff like last time. I do not like smiley faces on my *empanadas*."

As Kelley begin to put small fork holes in each pastry so that they could breath in the oven, she realized that this dish was usually for special occasions.

"Maria, why the *empanadas* tonight? What's up?"

Maria was rinsing out the mixing bowls at the sink. "The gardener said he loved them so I thought it would be a nice thing to do for the man. You know he's staying in the guest house, and we are feeding him, right?"

It hadn't occurred to Kelley that Maria would have talked to the gardener, but Maria was originally from Mexico so she probably loved a chance to speak Spanish. She had moved out here when her husband was killed in Vietnam in the sixties. Maria told Kelley once that she just couldn't sit in their apartment in Brooklyn; it was too

31

depressing. She didn't want to go back to Mexico, even though she missed her family, so she struck out on her own, using her cooking skills to find work.

"So what's the gardener like?" asked Kelley.

"He's very nice, very smart. And he knows good food if he knows about *empanadas*," Maria said smiling. "You should go talk to him sometime."

"Sure," said Kelley offhandedly. "Hey, Maria, speaking of talking to someone, I have a strange request."

"What is it *mija*?"

"Well, for English class we're supposed to talk to someone about quotes the teacher's giving us. Tonight he said it had to be a family member. Can I run it by you?"

Maria stopped scrubbing and turned around. "Why don't you ask your mother?"

Kelley looked down at the filled pastries, thinking.

"Well, *mija*, go give her a chance before you make up your mind."

Kelley set the fork down. "Okay, I guess the sooner the better."

As she walked through the long hallway, she called out "Mom" but got no answer. She found her back on the sun porch, curled up in the big wicker chair, asleep. A full martini sat on the wrought iron table.

Kelley looked at her mom in the glow of the setting sun. Her face looked thin and sallow. She has aged so much, she thought. She's just fifty. Is it the drinking? And why did she start drinking so much a few months ago? The arguments with dad were nothing new, but the ferocity, the meanness, the bile they threw at each other had intensified. A recurring thought entered her head— my parents are headed for a divorce. A knot filled her stomach.

Kelly turned to look out the window. Under the tree squatted the new gardener, staring down at a large sheet of white paper. Well, she thought, I gotta' ask someone about this quote. Chris will be no help when he gets home. If my teacher asks I'll just tell him I asked a member of the family of man.

She pushed open the sun porch door and walked across the yard. Alison had never had anything planted in the back yard since the initial grass seeding. It looked very much like the prairie it had once been. The huge tree arched over everything near the rear of the yard. Kelley loved that tree. She didn't know what kind it was, but it kept most of its short oval leaves all year. She bent down to pick up one. As she turned it over in her hands, she realized how it resembled the shape of an *empanada*. Kelley walked up behind the man sitting by the large trunk of the tree and looked over his shoulder.

"Wow!" she exclaimed.

The man turned around and smiled.

"That's beautiful!" Kelly said, staring down at a drawing of a Japanese garden. A stream with small waterfalls led from the upper-left corner of the yard down to the right, past the base of the tree, then made a curve like the belly of a pregnant woman, circling back to a small pond near the bottom of the picture by the deck outside of the sun porch. Tall reeds had been drawn in along the stream. Outside the reeds, a rich leafy ground cover extended outwards. Beyond this were low evergreens, then bamboo running along the redwood fences. Inside the "belly" section were five large black stones surrounded by a pond of white pebbles raked into concentric lines.

"Thank you," said the little man.

33

Kelley stared at the sparkle deep in his chocolate brown eyes.

"I'm sorry," she said. "I'm Kelley. I live here."

The man stood up. He was about the same height as Kelley.

"A pleasure to meet you," he said extending his hand.

She shook it, feeling the calluses on the inside of his fat fingers.

"Are you going to be able to get all that done in two weeks."

He glanced down at the paper, then back up to her, smiling.

"Why not? If I take my time in the beginning and ask the right questions, it will all fall into place."

"Why do you have to ask questions?" she thought out loud. "I mean, you seem to know what you're doing."

The man smiled. "Well, when I start by asking questions, I actually discover more questions, but then I begin to see which questions are the most important. Once I know that, I can discover what must be done first, making less mistakes."

"Do you really need to do all that?" she replied with skepticism.

The gardener chuckled. "May I tell you a little story about what happens when you don't ask questions?"

"Sure."

"Well, one time a kindergarten teacher noticed one of her little boys just staring at his boots when it was time to go out for recess. She went over to help him. The teacher picked up the right boot and the boy grabbed the small chair as she struggled to push the boot on. By the time she got the second boot on, the boy whimpered, 'Mrs. Kennedy, they're on the wrong feet.'

"Mrs. Kennedy looked down and sure enough they were. So she struggled now to get them off. She reversed the boots and told the boy to grab his chair again as she began pushing the boots back on. It didn't go any easier. When she finally got them on, the boy looked up and said, 'Mrs. Kennedy, these aren't my boots.'

"Exasperated Mrs. Kennedy asked him why he hadn't said so. The boy was frightened now so remained silent.

"Mrs. Kennedy began the struggle again, pulling the boots off while the boy clung for dear life to the chair. Once she got them off she looked up at the boy to ask him where his boots were. But before she opened her mouth the boy said, 'They're my brother's boots. My mother made me wear them.'

"Mrs. Kennedy's head fell to her chest; she put her hand up to her forehead, covering her eyes. Just take deep breaths, she thought. Okay, one more time. She straightened up and told the boy to grab the chair. A drop of perspiration splattered on the second boot as it finally went on. She looked up at the boy and asked, 'Now, where are your mittens?'

'I stuffed them inside the boots.' he replied."

Kelley burst into laughter.

"Oh my god! That's so funny!"

The man smiled, watching her laugh.

"That was great. Really. Hey, can you help me with an assignment?"

"I can try," he said.

"Well this teacher gave us a quote we're supposed to talk about with someone. Will you look at it?"

"Sure," he said.

Kelley pulled the scrap of paper out of her back pocket.

"Okay, the quote is *'Many do not think about the things they experience, nor do they know the things they learn; but they think they do.'* It's by somebody called Hera, Heara . . ."

"Heraclitus," interrupted the man.

Kelly looked up at him wide-eyed.

"Yea, that's right. So what do you think it means?"

"What do you think it means?" he responded.

Kelley looked down at the paper, her lips moving as she reread.

"I don't know. I guess that maybe people just go about life without questioning stuff. They just kind of accept things as they are. And that you need to ask questions to learn about things more deeply."

Kelley looked up at the man.

"Unlike certain kindergarten teachers," she said , smiling.

"And like certain gardeners," the man said winking.

She laughed at that.

"Yea, I get it. Thanks." She reached out to shake his hand again. "What's your name by the way?"

"I'm Luis."

**Music: "Down to Zero" sung by Joan Armatrading.
For Steve Carlson**

Chapter 3

Week One, Day Three

And as ye would that men should do to you,
do ye also to them likewise.

--Luke 6:31, the Bible

Bradford picked up the stack of contracts, tapping them down on the desk to straighten up the pile. The phone rang.

"Hello, All American Mortgage. This is Bradford. How can I put you in a new home?"

He grimaced when he heard the foreign accent.

"Okay, *uno momento, por favor,*" he stuttered, then covered the phone mouthpiece.

"Juanita, this one's for you," he called across the small office. "Reel him in now, Juanita."

Juanita, sitting in the last desk on the right, immediately picked up the phone and began speaking Spanish.

No sooner had he set the receiver down that it rang again. Jesus, he said to himself. When it rains, it pours.

"Hello, All American Mortgage. This is Bradford. How can I put you in a new home?"

He listened intently. It sounded like an older woman on the line.

"Yes, M'am. That's right. Interest rates are at an all time low. And in fact, we can even get you a rate lower than the prime."

"Is it safer than your retirement money market fund? M'am, the price of houses *always* goes up, doesn't it?" He waited for her yes.

"M"am, excuse me, may I ask your name?"

He wrote down Mrs. Kowalski on an application form.

"Is there a Mr. Kowalski?"

"Oh, sorry to hear that, m'am. If you don't mind me asking, do you know your present interest rate on those money market funds?"

"Five percent!" he said in mock surprise.

"M'am, if you were to get an interest-only loan for a new home, even if you hold onto the home for only a year, you'd be able to sell if for thousands in profit."

Bradford swiveled around to the computer. "Excuse me, Mrs. Kowalski. Would you mind giving me your address?"

He typed it and in seconds the GPS program identified her neighborhood and street. The street was lined with apartment buildings.

"So, I gather you're renting now, right?"

"Well, m'am, at All American we make it a point to know our neighbors and our neighborhoods. Now I'm guess you're paying about nine hundred to twelve hundred in rent, right?"

"Oh, that much! Well Mrs. Kowalski, your present rent will easily cover your interest-only monthly payments. I'd say we can have you in a brand new home by the end of the month!"

"Yes, seriously! Look, give me your Social Security number, and I'll run a quick credit check."

"Yes m'am, I know they say you shouldn't give your Social Security number over the phone, but that's to people who call you and try to get it out of you. You called us, and we're a mortgage company."

Bradford brought up another screen and typed in her number. So, she's seventy-four years old. Decent credit score.

"M'am, by any chance are you around later this afternoon?"

"Well yes, it could be after you watch the evening news at six. We just don't want to miss out on these low interest rates. Let me send one of our mortgage accountants over to you with your credit scores and the applications. He can answer every question you have. We have tons of properties that you'd qualify for, and he can bring pictures of them up on the computer for you to see."

"Yes, that's right. Right there in your own living room. Mrs. Kowalski, you may be able to pick out your new house tonight!"

Bradford heard a small gasp on the phone.

"How about six-thirty, right after the news?"

"Six forty-five is fine. His name is Mr. Jackson. He'll be wearing one of our blazers so you'll know that it's him."

"No m'am. We thank you!"

Bradford hung up the phone. Since deregulation it had never been easier to make money. The Securities and Exchange Commission had all but disappeared under the present administration, and Congress was protecting the big banks.

"Anita," he called back to a lady sitting a few desks away. "Get hold of Jackson and tell him he's due at the address I'm emailing you at six forty-five."

"I think Mike has his son's Little League game today," responded Anita, looking up concerned.

39

"Anita, Mr. Jackson is playing in the Big Leagues now so he better have his butt over there at six forty-five."

*   *   *   *   *

Alison pushed open the sun porch door and walked barefoot towards the gardener who was by the base of the tree. The grass felt so cool and soft under her feet. It's been so long since I walked barefoot in the grass, she thought.

She had watched the gardener bend over this large sheet of paper all yesterday and throughout the morning.

He turned when he heard her coming.

"You have very good timing, Mrs. Sparks," he said smiling.

"I'm glad someone feels I have good timing, Luis. So, show me what you have."

The gardener moved over to the right and patted the grass. Alison looked at him in disbelief. He couldn't possibly want her to sit in the grass in her Chanel sun dress. He stared up at her and patted the ground again. What the hell, she thought, if the grass feels good on my feet, it'll feel good on my butt. She lowered herself down, pulling the dress over her knees as she sat cross-legged. She leaned over to look at the plan.

"My goodness!" she exclaimed. "You're quite the artist!"

The gardener smiled broadly.

"I wondered why you were taking so long. Why, you've drawn a picture of the way the yard will look, plants and all. They're even labeled: nandena, sword and asparagus ferns, dwarf Japanese red maples," she read aloud.

Alison bent over closely, examining the details. She placed her finger on the stream and followed it toward the house, all the way to the small pond.

"What are these spotted orange fish in here?"

"Koi," he said, looking at her as she stared at the drawing. She looked concerned.

"Don't worry, Mrs. Sparks. They will be fine in this climate."

"Well, it's really something. But seriously, can we do all this in two weeks? I mean, this is a lot of work for one man."

"Well, I will have help. We'll need to get a backhoe in here tomorrow to grade the lawn and dig the stream and pond. That means on Friday we can have the irrigation and lighting lines placed. The stone could be delivered on Saturday. I've already calculated the amounts and will call the stone company before they close today."

"But who's going to plant all these plants?" she said starting to count the figures on the drawing.

He waited until she had reached thirty-five and paused.

"I will," he replied confidently.

"You must love your work," she said sarcastically.

"Well, yes, I do love gardening. Perhaps you know the old saying, 'You can bury a lot of troubles digging in the dirt.'"

Allison laughed.

"But I think work in general is a good thing, Mrs. Sparks. People need a purpose," continued Luis.

"Really?" she said with disbelief. "Then why do most people spend their life trying to get out of it?"

"I imagine those who try to get out it do not love what they are doing, but those that have found passion in their work, well, they have found their bliss."

Alison looked at him, unconvinced. Luis leaned in towards her.

"May I tell you an old story, Mrs. Sparks?"

She nodded yes.

"Well, a man died and suddenly found himself in a very beautiful place. A servant walked up and told him that he could have anything he chose, whether it be sustenance or pleasure. Well, the man was delighted. For days he immersed himself in every treat and treasure he could think of.

"After about a week, however, he found himself getting bored. He asked the servant to give him something to do. The servant replied 'There is no work for you here.'

"The man was shocked. 'Well, I might as well be in hell,' he yelled.

'Where do you think you are?' the servant replied."

Alison had been staring at the paper throughout the story. She sat in quiet now, as did the gardener.

After a couple of minutes she straightened herself up. Her eyes were brimming with tears.

"What have I become?" she said quietly.

"Mrs. Sparks, you are the person who is helping create a beautiful garden."

"Thank you. You're very kind," she said, patting Luis's arm. "But I think I've lost my way. I once had such dreams, such drive. I had huge goals."

"Will you help me then?" asked Luis.

Alison spun her head to face him. "You mean, me! Oh don't be silly! Get out here with a shovel and dig holes in the ground?"

"I asked if you would help me," replied the gardener. "What you choose to do is up to you."

Alison stared at this strange little man.

"I don't know," she said, shaking her head from side to side.

Luis leaned over his plans. "Hmm," he mumbled. "Two weeks. Maybe I should take out the pond."

Alison turned to him, her right eyebrow arched and a wicked smile on her face.

"Okay, okay, but only if you have an extra pair of gloves. I am *not* ruining these nails."

Music: "Stuck in a Moment" sung by U2.
For the Sparks Family

43

Chapter 4

Week One, Day Four

To love oneself is the beginning of a lifelong romance.

--Oscar Wilde

Kelley found Sasha where they always met before first period after a heavy homework night, at the far corner table in the library. She was texting on her cell when Kelley walked up. Kelley pulled out the one piece of homework she still hadn't finished.

Sasha giggled, typed "**ttyl**" and shut her phone.

"Hey, what's up?" she said, taking in Kelley's outfit. "You look good in that green blouse girl! You and that red hair can like wear all kinds of cool colors. You might as well be Irish. Hey, I'm thinking of getting a weave!"

Kelley's mouth dropped open.

"You are not!" she whispered loudly.

"Why not?" she said, pulling at her hair. "Hey, did you get your part of AP History done? Here's a copy of my part."

"Yea, here's my part," said Kelley, pulling a stack of paper out of her backpack. "Now I just need time to read your notes before class."

"Well, we *could* study now," said Sasha grinning.

"Uh uh," said Kelley. "Not til I hear about your argument with Peyton last night. You cannot text me about a fight right before I go to sleep and expect me to forget it."

"Oh, you know, Kelley. It's the same old crap from Peyton. When we gonna' do it? When we gonna' do it?" she sang sarcastically.

"I swear," said Kelley. "It's all boys have on their minds, that and football. Somebody ought to invent a pill for it."

The girls laughed at that.

"What did you tell him?"

"Oh, like he wants to do it this weekend at the big party at the Hazelton's on Saturday."

"*At the party!*" exclaimed Kelley.

"Well, the Hazelton's are gone for the weekend and the party will like be totally wild. Todd has told him we could use his room."

"Sasha, do you wanna' do it?"

Sasha buried her head in her hands. "Well hell, Kelley, like we've got to do it sometime," she said defensively. "Everyone else has. Are we gonna' die virgins? I mean, l do like Peyton."

Kelley sat back in her seat. She had felt the same pressure so many times. Here she was getting ready to go to college and she still hadn't had sex with a guy. She and Sasha had dated a number of good looking guys, but both had sworn years ago they wouldn't do it until they knew they were in love. So while their classmates talked of birth control and hot sex, Sasha and Kelley joked about chastity belts.

"Sasha, I can't tell you what to do, but just promise you'll make him use a condom, okay?"

"Uh, duh!" whispered Sasha. "Like I wanna' pick up some creepy diseases. So, like you gonna' come this Saturday?"

"I don't know. I want to, but my brother will be there getting smashed with all the jocks. It bugs me to see him trying so hard to be liked, especially by the older guys. Every time we're at a party together I find myself avoiding him."

"Kel! Look, the Hazelton's house is humongous. You can like hang out in an entirely different part of the house. They'll all be in the den where Todd's father's bar is anyway. Come on," she said whining. "We'll have fun!"

"*We'll* have fun," mocked Kelley. "Girl, you'll be upstairs doing it, and I'll be downstairs avoiding it."

"Come on, Kel," pleaded Sasha.

Kelly pulled her incomplete English assignment in front of her.

"Maybe," she said. "Hey, can you help me with something?"

Sasha leaned over and saw the quote at the top of the page.

"Oh god, not this quote thing again. I mean, like hasn't your teacher run that in the ground already?"

"Come on, Sasha. Just read it and tell me what you think."

Sasha smiled. "Okay, pass it here."

Kelley slid the paper across the table, and Sasha read the quote aloud.

"To love oneself is the beginning of a lifelong romance. Oscar Wilde"

"Hmmm, sounds to me like half the seniors on the football team," she said. The girls burst into laughter.

The sound of 'Shhhhh' came from the librarian's desk and both of them ducked their heads, giggling.

"Really, what's your take on it?" asked Kelley.

"Well, I guess if you think you're pretty amazing, and no one tells you any different, you'll believe it your whole life. I mean, look at Chase. He was born with a silver spoon in his mouth. And he certainly seems like he's in love with himself."

Kelley stared at the paper.

"Maybe it doesn't mean loving oneself in a bad way. Maybe it means just accepting yourself for the way you are. So you're not always wanting to be someone else."

Sasha looked puzzled. "Whatever."

The bell rang and the girls shoved their work in their knapsacks. Both clicked open their phones as they headed into the hallway.

*   *   *   *   *

First period football study hall was a different experience every day. Chris learned quickly that it depended on which coach lost the draw and had to oversee it. Coach Howell took study hall as seriously as his pre-AP History class. If he was there, you kept your nose in your books and didn't dare say a word, or it was laps at practice. If Coach Sutton was there, you could do whatever you wanted but you had to stay in your seat. Coach Nedza was a bit trickier. He'd make you study unless you got him talking about himself. Consequently, players chatted softly with each other but kept one ear on what Nedza was saying. As soon as they heard him end one story, some player would ask for another. Nedza never paid attention to where players sat so you could move around everyday.

Chris walked into study hall and saw Coach Nedza sitting behind the desk. Excellent, he thought. He quickly spotted Chase with an empty seat behind him. He hurried down the aisle and slid in the desk behind the first string quarterback.

Chase McDaniel was six foot four. He had jet black hair, blue eyes, and shoulders so broad Chris wasn't sure how he got through classroom doors. He had been physically ahead of his classmates his entire life, thus he found it easy to excel around them. He even got decent grades, especially for someone who did as little studying as possible. He got his brains from his parents. His dad was an executive with one of the pharmaceutical companies, and his mom was a chemist. Chase knew he'd get a football or basketball scholarship somewhere so he didn't feel the pressure that most students endured to get into a good school, or worse, one of their parents' alma maters.

Samuels, a defensive tackle, already had Nedza going on about his college days. Chris opened his math book but waited for a break in Chase's conversation with Davis on his right. They were talking about one of the hottest girls on campus that they both swore they had had. From the details of their conversation Chris believed them.

Chris had been dating Suzanne since he met her over the summer at the country club pool. She was on the school swim team and had an unbelievable body, but he hadn't made much progress with her besides pizza dates and making out. He'd just got his license though and expected his girl experiences to get radical soon. Suzanne seemed definitely interested in him, and she was lots of fun to be around, making him laugh all the time. She had memorized a bunch of George Carlin's one-liners and she would blurt them out whenever things got dull. Lines like:

"Why are a wise man and a wise guy opposites?"
"If love is blind, why is lingerie so popular?"

"When cheese gets its picture taken, what does it say?"

"If a cow laughed, would milk come out her nose?" and Chris's favorite since it involved his father:

"Why is the man who invests all your money called a broker?"

Chase swung around suddenly and spotted Chris.

"Hey little man," he called. "When did you sneak in?"

"Hey, Chase. Well, you know I'm pretty stealthy. That's how I'm gonna' steal your position."

Chase laughed. "So, what's up?"

"Nothing much, getting excited about the party Saturday night," he said closing his math book.

"Oh yea, man. You gonna' be giving it to that swimmer chick. What's her name, Tammy?"

"Suzanne. Her name is . . ."

"Whatever," Chase interrupted. "So man, is she going to the party Saturday night?"

Chris nodded yes.

"Well, you know the Hazelton's have an Olympic-size pool. You need to get her out there and practice your breast stroke." Chase laughed at his joke. Chris smiled.

Breast stroke, he thought. I've never even touched one. He decided to take a chance.

"Hey Chase. Can I ask you a private question?"

Chase's eyes glimmered. He leaned in. "Sure man, hit me with it."

"So, like it's kind of embarrassing."

"Come on, man. Just tell me." Chase said impatiently and started to turn around.

Chris grabbed his sleeve and leaned in.

"Okay, but this is private. You see, well, it's just that I really haven't gotten that far with a girl yet. So maybe you could tell me how I broach the subject."

"Broach the subject?" Chase said loudly.

"Shhhh, man!" Chris hissed.

"You mean you're a virgin?" Chase said laughing.

"No, man. Don't!" Chris pleaded.

"Hey, Davis. Our little third stringer here is still a virgin."

Davis looked up from his iPhone. "Bud, what's up with that?'" he said mockingly. "Here Chase, this will teach him something."

Davis handed Chase his cell. Chase looked at it and laughed.

"Oh yea, this is a good one." He turned to Chris and handed him the phone. "Now you study this real good little man and you'll be ready for Saturday night." Chase turned around and began laughing with Davis.

Chris looked down at the screen on the iPhone. A girl was lying naked on a bed with three guys in boxers around her. He'd seen it before too.

"Here man," he said, handing him the phone back. He opened his math book. Jesus, I should have known better, he thought.

*   *   *   *   *

Bradford didn't hear the noise at first. As he pulled into the driveway he had "Sweet Home, Alabama" blaring on the Blaupunkt surround-sound stereo in the Escalade. He always spent a moment in his car when he got home, thinking about his day, how well he was doing, how rich he was getting. Too bad his old man had never been around. He'd like to rub some of this money in his face

50

right now. Today, Thursday, had been a little rough though. Interest rates had been rising for a few months now, home ownership was already at record levels, and prices were beginning to drop. Home owners were finding it hard to refinance. The stock market was getting nervous and had dropped over 300 points today. Credit was starting to tighten up. No worries, he thought. We're still finding lots of buyers, and as long as the banks continue to buy our loans, I make money, big money.

When the song ended, he switched off the car. Suddenly he heard a loud roaring sound from the backyard. What the hell? he thought.

Jumping out of the SUV, his feet hit the gravel running as he hurried around the end of the house. He couldn't believe his eyes. The backyard was completely torn up. A backhoe had dug a trench from the far left corner across the middle of the yard, then turned back scouring the earth parallel with the sun porch. The operator jerked the levers so that the claw dug a huge scoop of dirt out and dropped it into the back of a pickup. Standing at the age of the yard with their backs to him were Alison, Kelley, and Chris, watching as the huge scoop tore through the earth again.

"What the hell is going on?" he yelled.

Only Chris heard him and turned around. He hunched his shoulders, indicating he had no clue. Chris then tapped Kelley who turned, saw him, and then tapped Alison. Alison turned halfway around, a martini in her hand.

Bradford stomped towards them. "What happened? A pipe break? Jesus!"

Alison looked at him calmly. "No, my dear. It's our new Zen garden. See how peaceful it already is," she said sarcastically.

Bradford was fuming. "Who said you ...."

Before he could finish she held up her hand in his face. She looked directly into his eyes and said coolly. "We are having a new garden, Bradford. Get over it."

He stared at her, at the backhoe as it took another chunk of soil near the base of his tree.

"Alison, if anything happens to that tree, I'll kill you."

"Don't worry, Bradford. The tree stays. It's part of the plan."

Bradford spread his hands out to the backyard. "Alison, do we have to dig up the entire yard? Can't we just plant some shrubs, ferns, put in a bird bath? I mean, do we have to do all this, spend all this money?"

Alison smiled. "We've planned a beautiful Japanese garden, Bradford. But the gardener said it is important to put in the proper infrastructure. I agreed and signed off on it."

Bradford' turned to face her. "I told him to just pull weeds!"

"And I told him to build me a beautiful garden."

Bradford shook his head. "Where is he?"

"He's gone to pick out the stones that arrive on Saturday."

Bradford's shoulders dropped. He knew he wasn't going to win this one. "Is this what he said to do then?" he said more calmly, pointing at the torn up yard.

Alison suddenly laughed and took a sip of martini. "Well no, he actually quoted Thoreau."

"Thoreau?" Bradford yelled.

Alison picked the olive out of the glass. "Yes, let's see. I think he said, 'If you have built castles in the air, your work need not be lost; that is where they should be. Now put the foundations under them.'"

Bradford shook his head and spun around to go inside. He saw Maria smiling broadly at the kitchen window.

"Maria, get off your lazy butt and get me some dinner!" he yelled as he headed inside.

Maria burst into laugher.

Music: "Sitting" sung by Cat Stevens.
For Chris and Kelley

Chapter 5

Week One, Day Five

Our prime purpose in this life is to help others.
And if you can't help them, at least do not harm them.

--The Dalai Lama

Maria sliced the goat cheese and sun dried tomato frittata in large pieces. She always tried to make something special for the kids on Friday. Last week it was fresh blueberry pancakes for Kelley, who only allowed herself half of one, but she loved them. Chris came bounding into the kitchen, saw the frittata and gave Maria a big hug.

"You made me frittata for football," he exclaimed.

"I made you frittata," said Marie. "You make your own football."

Chris's face fell at the football comment and he took his seat at the kitchen table.

Feeling a little guilty, Maria asked. "So, who are you playing?"

Chris brightened as he pushed some bread down into the toaster. "Tarrytown. They're not very good, only won one game."

Maria knew why this was important. She ambled over to the table with the frittata. "Choose," she said pointing with a pie server. Chris pointed to a large slice. "Do you think you'll get to play?" she asked as she plopped the piece on his plate.

"I could," he said excitedly. "If we run up the score high enough, Coach will play most everyone."

Kelley came into the kitchen, put her arm around her brother and stuck her tongue in his left ear.

"Eeewwwww!" he yelled.

"Love lick," she said laughing.

Chris wiped his ear out with the napkin. "Hey Kel, you *are* gonna' come to the game tonight, right?"

Kelley put her hand to her chin like she was thinking. "Hmmm. Well, I do have that modeling job for Vanity Fair, but I guess I can cancel it."

Chris opened his mouth full of frittata and said "Seafood!"

"You're a pig," said Kelley, grabbing one of his pieces of toast as it popped up.

"So, you think you're gonna' get to play?"

"Maybe. It's Tarrytown, and they suck."

Bradford walked into the kitchen with his briefcase, attired in his uniform—blue All American Mortgage blazer, white shirt, red tie. He set his briefcase down in his chair. Maria knew what this meant; he was not stopping for breakfast.

"Mr. Sparks, how about a nice piece of frittata? Sit for a second."

"Can't, Maria. Thanks," he said pulling out his Blackberry, or Crackberry, as Kelley and Chris called it because of its addictive nature.

"Damn!" he said. "Market is falling again."

He reached for his briefcase.

"Dad?" said Chris looking up at his father. "We play Tarrytown tonight."

His dad looked back at his Blackberry. "Great son. Hope you win."

"You gonna' come?" Chris asked hopefully. "There's a good chance . . . ."

"Look son, we've been through this before. When you become first string, I'll come to a game. But now you need to focus on goals that are going to get you somewhere. You're always asking me for new clothes, a new iPhone, a new car. How do you think you're going to pay for these when you're older? You and I know you're not going to be a football star." Bradford paused for a moment, studying his son sitting in front of him. "Did you see the book I left on your bed?"

"I saw it, dad." Chris said dejectedly.

"What's the title then?" his dad challenged.

Chris looked him in the eyes. "How to Get Into the Top MBA Schools."

"Good, at least you read the title. Now read some more. Competition is stiff for those slots, and I guarantee you some kids are already way ahead of you." He slid his Blackberry in his inside coat pocket and picked up his briefcase. Maria had wrapped up a piece of frittata in aluminum foil and turned to hand it to him, but Bradford was already past her, hurrying out the garage door.

Kelley looked across the table at her brother. His face displayed a mixture of hurt and hate.

"Chris," she said. Chris turned to look at her. She pointed at her heart. "Fifty yard line, buddy."

*   *   *   *   *

Mr. Doty always stood at the door and greeted his students as they entered each of his classes. A short bald man, many of the students, especially the football players, towered over him. In fact, last week Klemp, the six-four defensive linebacker, was at the chalkboard beside Mr.

Doty, who had his students pantomiming poems. Klemp looked down at Doty's bald head and pretended to fix his hair. No one laughed any harder than Mr. Doty. He told Klemp that he would begin charging him "grooming rights" next week.

When everyone had taken their seats, Mr. Doty let out a deep groan. The students had been talking amongst themselves, and all grew silent and turned towards him in their seats.

"Mr. Doty, are you all right?" asked Malia.

"Yes, I'm fine. I was just thinking that if I gave a big groan before I asked you to talk about today's quote, you wouldn't have to."

The students pelted Doty with groans.

"Okay, okay. Who wants to start, or do I do the random finger down the grade book selection process?" he said, picking up the grade book. There were no takers. He opened the book to second period AP English, closed his eyes, raised his hand above his head, made three swirling motions and the sound of a dive bomber, then planted his finger on the page.

"Kelley Sparks!" he called out.

Kelley couldn't believe it. The one night she had not asked anyone about a quote, and she gets called on first. All heads turned to Kelley. She looked down at her notebook to give the appearance of having written something down.

"Well, . . ." she said stalling.

Doty smiled. "Okay, Kelley. I'll read it aloud to give you time to come up with an answer. '*Our prime purpose in this life is to help others. And if you can't help them, at least do not harm them.*'"

Kelley straightened in her seat. "Well, being that it's from the spiritual leader of Tibet, it reminds me of the

Bible verse that tells us to turn the other cheek. In other words, we should go through life not harming others." She looked up at Mr. Doty for affirmation.

Mr. Doty walked down the aisle towards her seat. "Did anyone get a different opinion?"

Jefferson Samuels raised his hand.

"Well, Mr. Samuels, tell us your opinion."

"Mr. Doty, I think this is a little nutty. I mean, this guy is a spiritual leader. When you're a spiritual leader you see everything as black or white. It's easy to be removed from the real world and say that we should never harm anyone. I mean, really, isn't that his job?"

"So, Mr. Samuels, you're saying that this quote doesn't really apply to the real world."

Samuels leaned back in his seat. "Yea, I think so. I mean, I play football. I'm a defensive back. My job is to put a hurt on somebody."

Andrew Jenks, another football player sitting beside Samuels, applauded and banged fists with his friend.

"Okay, then is any spiritual leader like the Dalai Lama speaking of the real world?" asked Mr. Doty.

Dina Park, an Asian student who was normally quiet, raised her hand.

"Yes, Dina," said Doty, surprised but excited that she wanted to contribute.

"Mr. Doty, I don't think the Dalai Lama is wrong. I think Jefferson's context is wrong. You see, a game or sport is something that people agree to join and also agree to follow a set of rules. None of us agreed to join life; we were simply brought into it. And the rules vary from culture to culture, from country to country, from community to community. I think the Dalai Lama is talking about our daily lives, not our manufactured games."

"Jefferson?" asked Mr. Doty.

Jefferson, who had been staring at Dina, turned to Mr. Doty. "I'll give her that one, Mr. Doty. The player opposite me on the field knows the rules, and he's planning to hurt me too. That is *if* he can!" he said straightening up in his seat and grinning broadly.

A hand went up on the right side of the room. "Mr. Doty, aren't we just talking about the value of non-violence here?" stated Larry, a counter-culture student who often wore black clothing and Buddha beads on his wrist.

"Can you explain more?" asked Doty.

Larry leaned intently over his desk. "Well, it's Gandhi isn't it. He brought down the British Empire and its imperialistic control of India by simply deciding not to do any harm."

Hands shot up around the room.

"Rebecca," said Mr. Doty.

"Gandhi did change a nation, and he did tell his followers not to use physical violence, but you can't say that he didn't cause any harm. Whether you liked the British or not, Gandhi forced their removal from the country. Lives were disrupted. I mean, is it really possible to never do anyone harm when things change?"

Kelley raised her hand quickly.

"Yes, Ms. Sparks?"

"Mr. Doty, sometimes we do harm and we don't mean to, or even know it. Wasn't there some group back in ancient times who tried not to hurt any living thing? Like they would brush ants from in front of their path so that they didn't step on them?"

"No way!" called out Jefferson.

"The Jainists, Ms. Sparks. Yes, that was there philosophy," answered Mr. Doty.

"What a silly way to live!" said Jefferson.

"Anything is silly if you take it to an extreme," called out Malia. The class turned to her. "I think the Dalai Lama is just telling us to be aware that we constantly have a choice of how we treat others. Maybe it would do us all a little good to go through the day considering how we were going to treat the next person we met."

"Testify, girl!" called out Martin from the back.

The discussion continued for another fifteen minutes until Mr. Doty suggested a break. He asked the class to open their literature anthology and read Gandhi's letter on non-violence. He then gave students ten seconds to find a partner and asked them to choose a side on the following debate topic: Nonviolence is a more effective means than violence to create societal change.

"Okay, we'll move in a minute to the computers around the room. You have the remainder of the period to look up sources to support your opinion. Remember, one of the factors judged on the AP exam is how well opinions are supported and that you acknowledge counter-arguments. So, you'll also need to look up opposing information to prepare for your opponents' attacks. I'll be watching to see who's working and who's playing. Tomorrow at the end of class we'll have one of our twenty-minute debates on the subject. I'll choose a pair that played around to face off against a pair that worked hard. So, if you don't want to be embarrassed in front of your peers, I suggest you go to work. Now!"

*   *   *   *   *

The game against Tarrytown was a rout as expected. Chase had thrown three touchdown passes and run for two before Coach Preston took him out in the fourth quarter. Chris was finally put in with four minutes left in the game. Coach was sending in the plays and his first one was a handoff to the half-back to the right. The second play was a handoff to the left. Thus far the team had gained four yards. Chris waited expectantly in the huddle for the player to run in the call. Please let me throw a pass, he thought.

The player ran in and called "17 Long." Chris smiled broadly. He repeated the call, broke the huddle, and walked up behind the center. Plant my back foot, he said to himself.

"Hut, hut, 42 − 21 − 17"

The ball slapped into his hands. He took his three steps back, planted and threw to where the end should be. Something huge slammed into him, and he was thrown to the turf on his back. A heavy weight rolled off of him, and he gasped for air but none went in. The center ran over, saw him struggling to breathe, and reached down and pulled his football pants away from his waist.

"Just breathe slowly, Chris. It'll come."

Slowly his lungs let the air seep in, and he was able to get to his feet with the help of two players. Coach Preston sent the second string quarterback in to take his place. He loped off the field, feeling defeated and embarrassed.

Tim, his favorite end, ran up.

"You all right, man? Boy, that linebacker blitzed and hit you running full speed. I don't think you ever saw him."

Chris looked at Tim. "Trust me, I didn't."

Tim patted him on the back. "Well anyway, great pass man!"

Chris looked up surprised. "What?"

Tim laughed. "Oh my god. That's too funny. You don't even know you completed your pass for a first down."

Chris grinned from ear to ear, shaking his head back and forth. He threw a completion and missed it. Crap!

As he walked over to the bench to get a cup of water, he looked up into the stands. There was Kelley, the only one standing, pointing first at him, and then at her heart.

"Way to go, you stud!" she yelled out.

Chris burst out laughing and gave her a thumb's up.

*   *   *   *   *

Bradford stared at the screen. He couldn't believe his eyes. It's a meltdown, he thought. Friday is always a sell-off day on the exchange so stocks normally fall, but this wasn't normal. The stock market had dropped another five hundred points. This meant a general loss of confidence, which meant panic selling, which meant the end of credit.

He had stayed behind at work late into the evening to watch the Asian markets as they opened. They were reacting just as expected. Since banking deregulation and globalization, most major banks were financially intertwined. If the Goldman Sachs and Lehman Brothers were getting hit, then most everyone would get hit.

Bradford felt an ache in his chest, almost a hollow deep hurt. This wasn't only his company that was in danger, it was his own portfolio. He had invested mostly in stocks and only a few mutual funds. All of his retirement was tied up in these assets. He could lose everything.

He turned off the computer and watched the glow of the blue screen diminish. He sat in the dark office, numb, lost.

**Music: "Superman" sung by Five For Fighting.
For Chris and Bradford**

Chapter 6

The Weekend

There are no wrong turns, only wrong thinking on the turns our life has taken.

--Zen saying

The stone arrived promptly at eight a.m. on Saturday. Luis guided the large truck back up to the edge of the yard. He had laid plywood down over the newly inserted electricity and irrigation lines wherever they would be moving the heavy rocks. Two large Hispanic men climbed out of the truck and smiled when they recognized Luis. They always enjoyed working with this man; he never went loco.

All the stone had been loaded on the truck exactly as Luis had requested. The large black rocks for the stone garden by the pond were loaded last so that the men could place them first. They shoved the smooth stones onto the truck's lift, lowered it down to the height of the wheelbarrow and rolled one in, then pushed the wheelbarrow over the plywood to the open space.

When all five stones were there Luis began placing them. He asked the men to move them again and again. They never complained, just waited and watched. Every time a stone was moved, Luis went inside the sun porch and sat in Mrs. Sparks' wicker chair to check that view. If he approved of that, he then walked to the other three compass points of the yard. If one angle did not appear "right" to him, the stones were moved again. Finally, after about an hour, he was satisfied.

Next the large bags of white quartz pebbles were unloaded—two three-hundred pound bags. These were carried over to the rock garden and broken open, then spread with rakes over the large circular surface to a depth of three inches. The black rocks now seemed to sprout out of the white pebbles—a stark but beautiful contrast.

At this point, Maria, who had been watching from inside the kitchen, brought out a pitcher of homemade lemonade for the crew. Under the shade of the tree, the men began telling stories in Spanish.

"So, mi amigos, did you hear about the young Mexican priest who was told he needed to go out into the country to bury an old hermit," asked Luis.

The two men shook their heads, smiling. One leaned back on his elbows, knowing a good story was coming.

"Well," continued Luis. "The funeral was to be held in a brand new cemetery way back in the country, and the hermit was to be the first man ever buried there. The priest, however, was not familiar with the area and got lost. He did not want to appear ignorant with his new parishioners, so he did not stop to ask for directions. Finally, the priest drove around a bend and saw a backhoe in a field near a house. The hearse was nowhere in sight. Two men, the digging crew, had stopped to eat lunch.

"The priest got out of his car and apologized for his tardiness, then stepped to the side of the open grave. He was surprised to see that the vault lid was already closed. He turned to the crew and told them to gather around; he would pray now. The two men moved obediently to the sides of the hole.

"The priest began to pour out his heart and soul for the lonely old man. He promised a brighter tomorrow and that glory would surely come. The workers began to say 'Amen,' 'Glory to God,' and 'Praise the Lord.' With the workers showing more interest, the priest became more inspired. He took off his coat and preached as he never had before, from Genesis to Revelations.

"When the priest had finally finished, he thanked the men and headed back to his car. As he climbed inside he heard one of the workers say to the other, 'I've never seen anything like that, and I've been putting in septic tanks for thirty years!'"

The men exploded into laughter and rolled back on the ground. After a few minutes, Luis slapped his knee and said "*Vamos*" and they headed back to work.

Next to come off the truck were the smaller boulders that would create the three small waterfalls in the stream as it traveled from the back of the yard, around the rock garden, and into the pond in front of the sun porch. Luis had reworked the ditch dug by the backhoe so that it had three one-foot drops. He had also lined it to retain the water and keep it from soaking into the soil. Luis placed the boulders at each of these points so that the water would cascade and create a rippling sound. To save water, he had also installed an underground pumping system that sent the water from the pond back up to the top of the stream.

Finally, the men began to unload the flat stone that would form the pathway and patio. One loaded the pieces off the truck; one carried the pieces to Luis by hand, and Luis patiently placed each one. If a stone seemed "wrong," he would set it aside and wait until the man brought him the "right" piece to fill a hole in the path. Working his way from the back of the yard, he extended the path to the future patio in front of the coach house. There he began laying the stones in a large rectangle. From the patio he then extended the path towards the house.

Allison had come outside and stood marveling at the creation of her garden. A smile was fixed on her face. She watched the stone pathway slowly approach her for nearly a half hour until the path reached the bend where it would continue to the sun porch door. She marveled at how much time Luis took to pick and place each stone, getting on his knees with a trowel and a level to make sure the stone was flat and secure. It was now late afternoon. The two men said goodbye and left Luis with the remaining stones by the driveway. Maria brought Allison out a chair and a glass of lemonade.

"Maria, I want to celebrate. Will you be a dear and make me a martini?"

Maria raised an eyebrow. "Ms. Sparks, I made you lemonade." She turned and went back inside the house.

Luis was now working almost in front of Allison. She watched him step back and stare at the two-foot wide path he had been building. Because each stone had its own unique shape, he had taken great care to create some type of visual harmony among the pieces.

"Luis?"

The little man turned, holding a rather large stone. "Yes, Mrs. Sparks? Do you like it?"

"Why yes, Luis, it's lovely. But personally I think you're spending an inordinate amount of time placing these rocks. I mean, it's such a little thing, and we have so much to do before next Saturday's competition."

Luis turned away, studied the ground for at least thirty seconds and then lowered the flat rock into its place. He turned back to Mrs. Sparks.

"Sometimes when I consider what tremendous consequences come from little things . . . I am tempted to think . . . there are no little things," he said, his brown eyes sparkling.

Mrs. Sparks laughed out loud and raised her glass of lemonade. "Hear, hear!" she said. "I gotta' give it to you, Luis, you do know little things."

Luis chuckled. "Not me, Mrs. Sparks. I borrowed that from Ralph Waldo Emerson."

*　　*　　*　　*　　*

By eight p.m. the Hazleton's driveway in front of their four-car garage was already filled with cars. Todd's parents were vacationing in the Grand Caymans. They had left his older sister, Heather, in charge of him and the house. She was a junior at the local branch of the state university. She had met her boyfriend at school and was deliriously in love with him. With her folks out of town, she had no intention of babysitting her brother. Her boyfriend was on the soccer team and had a midnight curfew, so she made a deal with Todd. He could do what he wanted Saturday night with two conditions: 1) he and his friends didn't wreck the house and 2) most everyone was gone by midnight when she came home.

Chris had been sitting by his front window waiting for an hour, tapping his foot. The Hazelton's lived only six blocks away, but he was not about to be seen walking up to the house. Finally at eight thirty Tim drove up. The Hazelton's driveway was already full when they arrived, and they had to park on the street.

Chris heard the music thumping from the sidewalk. This is going to be a blowout, he thought to himself. He walked into the foyer and looked into the living room where kids were sitting all over the furniture, plastic cups in hand, laughing and screaming. Tim had stopped to talk to a girl so he headed into the kitchen to find something to drink. The counters were lined with large bottles of liquor. Todd had invited older kids so that they could bring the booze. He quickly surveyed his choices: Vodka, Gin, Whiskey, Rum, Tequila, Schnapps and plenty of mixers. The favorite mixer among the students was an *"Energy"* drink full of caffeine. By mixing the two, kids got drunk quicker and didn't get tired so quickly. A large goldfish bowl on the counter was filled with cash donations. Chris pulled out a twenty and tossed it in. He planned to get his money's worth tonight.

The whir of a blender caught his attention. Carrie, a majorette, was working the buttons, changing the tone of the machine with each press. She flipped a glass over, dipping the edge in lime juice, then in salt, and then poured in a green frozen concoction.

"Hey, Chris!" she yelled. Chris was excited she knew his name. Suzanne's parents had not let her come to the party so he was a free man. Damn, he thought. She's hot. Carrie squeezed between two seniors who were trading shots of Cuervo.

"What's up?" said Chris.

Winking at one of the seniors, Carrie took a full shot from his hand and gave it to Chris.

"Let's get this party started," she sang, swinging her hips back and forth. Chris downed the shot and moved towards her, swinging his hips in time with her, just the way he had watched Chase do with other girls.

A hand landed on his shoulder, and he spun around to see Tim.

"Dude! You gotta' come see this. They got a double beer bong downstairs in the den. Come on, we got to get down there, man. The guys are lined up for it. Let's go."

Chris leaned over and gave Carrie a kiss on the cheek, then followed Tim through the crowd and down the stairs. He had seen pictures of beer bongs on college drinking Internet sites. As he entered the dimly lit room, he saw Todd standing on a chair holding a large funnel from which a plastic tube dangled. The tube ran into a plastic connector from which two tubes exited. Holding the long tubes were two football players.

"You guys ready?" said Todd. The two boys nodded and sat down on the floor, putting the tube ends in their mouths.

"Let's do it, man" yelled another boy in the room. A fourth boy popped a thirty-two ounce bottle of beer and handed it to Todd. He immediately began pouring the beer into the funnel. It flowed down the tube, dividing into two streams at the connector. When the beer got to the boys' mouths, someone yelled "Suck!"

Everyone cheered as the beer shot down the throats of the two boys sitting. One was able to swallow fast enough, but the other boy choked and sprayed beer all over himself. Boos erupted from the crowd.

Another pair of boys pushed the guys on the floor out of the way and grabbed the tubes. Todd was handed another bottle of beer. After two more pairs had their turns, it was Tim and Chris's chance. Chase had come downstairs. He stood watching with a large plastic cup in one hand. Bianca, a senior, held onto his arm. When he saw Chris and Tim sit down, he walked over to Todd standing in the chair and told him he wanted to do the pouring. Chris and Tim looked up, concerned. Chase turned to one of his best friends, Bart, and whispered something in his ear. Bart laughed, walked over to the table, and picked up a bottle.

Chase climbed onto the chair.

"Okay everybody, listen up!" he yelled. "Listen up! We've got two *boys* here who have yet to be initiated into the team, so we're going to give them a chance to show their stuff right now."

Cheers erupted in the room. Chris felt a hollow feeling in his stomach. He was trapped. He could not get up and leave. He caught the scared look in Tim's eyes.

"So," continued Chase. "We're going to give them a special Freeman Football Highball!" Everyone cheered again.

Chase looked down at the two boys sitting on the floor. "For your initiation, we're going to make you a special cocktail—beer and Russian vodka. Now, not only can you not spit out any, but you gotta' do three bongs in a row." Hoots and hollering filled the room.

"You ready, boys?"

Chris and Tim looked at each other, took a breath, and put the tubes up to their mouths. Bart held the funnel so that Chase could pour with both hands.

Chris looked up and saw the liquid coming. He shoved the tube in his mouth and tried to open his throat. The alcohol gushed into his mouth. He fought the urge to gag. He felt Tim kick as he struggled also. As quickly as it started, the liquid stopped. Tim and Chris triumphantly pulled the tubes from their mouths and held them up to cheers from everyone.

"Okay, boys. Here's number two!" yelled Chase. Bart handed him another bottle of beer. Chase had only used half a pint of vodka. Before the boys had time to catch their breath, he began pouring. Chris closed his eyes and opened his throat. The cold liquid shot down their throats again. Now the football players started clapping in time. Chase started his rap.

"Who's gonna' chug down number three?" he sang.

71

"Chris and Tim gonna' chug number three," called everyone. Chris's stomach felt bloated. He wasn't sure he could get down another but he knew he had to try. Tim let out a huge belch. Bart handed Chase another pint and a bottle of beer and took hold of the funnel. Chase immediately started pouring. Chris and Tim locked eyes and shoved the tubes in their mouths. This time Chris could feel the liquor back up, but he knew he couldn't let it out. He closed his eyes and forced his throat open. Suddenly the liquid stopped. Chris opened his eyes and there sat Tim, dry and smiling. They had done it! Their teammates cheered, pulled them up to their feet, and patted them on the back.

Chris heard words like, "totally awesome" and "rad" and "go Freeman ballers" as he found his legs, but his head was beginning to swim and his stomach felt queasy. Perhaps he should have eaten some lunch, he thought. He reached for Tim's arm and the two of them helped each other up the stairs.

"I think I need some fresh air, man," said Chris. "I'm going out to the pool."

Tim nodded, saying he needed to find a bathroom.

Chris wobbled through the huge house until he found a back door. He heard the sound of water splashing and walked towards it. Walking around a corner, he saw a huge pool with a water slide at one end. Six pairs of students were playing "chicken" in the pool. The boys loved this game because girls climbed onto their shoulders and tried to push the other pairs over. Seeing a lounge chair, Chris eased into it. He started to lie flat, but as soon as his head went horizontal, the world started spinning, and he felt a flood of nausea. Reaching back, he pulled the back of the seat up, felt it lock, closed his eyes and repeated over and over, "I will not throw up. I will not throw up."

*   *   *   *   *

Kelley headed over to the party around ten. She knew there was no need to get there until a number of students were drunk. As a junior, she had joined the school's Designated Driver Club. A couple of cheerleaders, concerned over how much they saw their classmates drinking, started the group three years earlier. They had done some research and discovered that at least seventy-five percent of high school seniors drank alcohol. Unfortunately, in such an affluent community, alcohol was only one of the commonly used drugs. Students in Farmington had easy access to ecstasy, cocaine, marijuana, and even crystal meth.

Sometimes the Designated Drivers, or DDers as they were also called, made driving appointments with particular students on party nights. They'd show up at an agreed upon time, convince the drunk students it was time to leave, and take them home. Since many parents drank in this community, they didn't mind their kids coming home a little drunk as long as they weren't driving.

Kelley walked into the Hazelton's house around ten. She scanned the living room for Chris. Not there. Walking into the kitchen, she squeezed through the crowd, asking kids if they'd seen her brother. One kid told her to check the basement. When she saw the beer bong, she knew the students were binge drinking.

She climbed the stairs and ran into Sasha.

"Oh my god," yelled Sasha, giving her a hug. "You came!"

Kelley laughed. "Well, I'm on duty, driving people home tonight."

"Kel, you're such a good person. So, like I guess you don't want a drink, huh."

Kelley laughed, then pointed to the plastic cup in Sasha's hand.

"So what are you drinking?"

Sasha winked at her. "Believe it or not it's a *Virgin* Bloody Mary."

Kelley's eyes widened. She had completely forgotten that this was the night that Sasha and Peyton might do it.

"Oh my god, Sasha, are you going to?"

Sasha laughed. "Well, I don't have to worry about that now. Peyton has been doing that bong thing in the basement and is like passed out on a bed upstairs."

"Wow. Are you disappointed?" asked Kelley.

"Nah, like actually I'm relieved."

"Cool," said Kelley, giving her a hug. "Listen, I just wanna' check on my little brother."

"Oh, well speaking of passed out . . . ."

"Oh no," groaned Kelley. "Where is he?"

"On a sun bed by the pool. He's okay. I checked on him. I mean he's breathing, but he isn't saying much."

"Sasha, thanks a bunch. Let me go get him."

Kelley walked back to the pool and there lay her little brother, sound asleep in his Ralph Lauren button down blue-striped shirt and khaki pants. One flip-flop dangled from his right foot. She gave him a nudge on his shoulder.

"Chris, wake up." He didn't respond.

"Chris," she said more loudly, giving him a little shake.

He was out. She couldn't stand to leave him here. He certainly wasn't in any condition to keep partying so she decided just to take him home.

Kelley walked over to the pool and asked two seniors to help her carry him to her car. Climbing out of the pool, the two muscular boys had no trouble picking Chris up. He groaned as they carried him. Kelley opened the passenger's side door, and they gently put him in. She rolled down his window so that the fresh air might wake him up.

By the time she pulled into the gravel driveway, Chris had leaned forward and put his head on the dash. Kelley stopped the car and realized she didn't know how she was going to get him inside. She reached over and gave him a good shake. Bad idea. Chris immediately threw up all over the floor board.

"Oh, Chris!" Kelley screamed. "Damn!"

She jumped out of the car. The smell of sour beer filled the air. Okay, she thought. I'll go inside and get rags and the pine-scented cleaner Maria uses. Pushing the button on the garage opener, she went inside. Chris kept a box of old towels in the corner that he used for washing and polishing his car. She began rummaging through them, picking those that she could later throw away. She couldn't find the cleaner. It had to be inside, she thought.

Kelley opened the door into the laundry room and began searching. She didn't have to worry about disturbing her parents. Around seven her mother had come home from a baby shower, tipsy, had another martini, and gone to her room. Her dad had come home just before Kelley left, griped about work, made himself a drink, and told her he was going to take a sleeping pill and not to bother him.

Kelley had just opened the cabinet above the washer when she heard the car start. "Oh, no!" she whispered. She bolted out the laundry door into the garage to see her car lurch forward, Chris at the wheel.

"Chris!" she screamed but he never heard her. He accelerated over the curb that bordered the driveway and plunged into the back yard. She ran around the corner of the house just in time to watch him hit the tree.

"No!" she yelled. Running to the car, she could hear the engine sputtering. Chris's head was leaning against the steering wheel. She yanked open the car door, and he started to roll out. As she reached to catch him, she realized he was too heavy for her. Suddenly another pair of large brown hands grabbed hold of Chris.

"I've got him," said a familiar voice.

Kelley looked up into the brown eyes of the gardener.

"Thank you, Luis," she said, panting for breath. Luis had heard the car hit the tree and run down from his room in the coach house.

"I'm not sure your brother should be driving tonight," he said smiling.

Kelley looked at Chris carefully to make sure he wasn't hurt. He had a small lump on his forehead but otherwise he seemed fine. The car couldn't have been going more than five miles an hour when he hit the tree.

Chris raised his head and tried to focus on Kelley. "Who the hell is driving?" he said drunkenly.

Kelley and Luis both laughed out loud.

"Let's take him to his room," said Luis. "You can look after him, and I'll handle everything out here."

"Thank you," said Kelley as she watched Luis lift Chris up and head toward the house.

*　　*　　*　　*　　*

Bradford rolled onto his left side and reached out but felt nothing. He opened his eyes. It had been four years since his wife left his bed, but he still found himself missing her. It felt so odd to sleep alone along the edge of the huge California King bed.

He rolled back to the right to check the time. Six a.m. Not bad, he thought. I actually slept eight hours. He decided to get up, get some coffee, and read the Sunday *NY Times* to see if there was any more information about this financial meltdown.

Sunday was Maria's day off so he filled the coffee maker with grounds and water himself. As the coffee began to percolate, he walked out through the garage to find the paper, which was usually lying on the carport or under one of the four cars. The paper was all the way by Chris's car. He reached down to pick it up, then heard the sound of someone digging. Looking up he saw the gardener out at the tree. Leading away from the gardener were two tire tracks running across the yard straight back to Kelley's car. He walked around the front of the car and saw the dent.

Kelley jumped in bed when her father banged on the door.

"Make yourself decent, young lady. We've got something to talk about."

Kelley pulled the sheet over her. This won't be much protection, she thought.

"Okay, come in."

Bradford threw the door open and marched over to her bed.

"What the hell happened last night?"

Kelley stared at him, not sure how to answer.

77

"Did you lose control of the car? Were you drinking? Answer me!" he bellowed.

"No, dad. I didn't."

"You hit my tree!" he yelled.

Kelley said nothing.

"Listen up, young lady. If you can't drive properly, you won't use the car. You won't be needing it anyway because you're grounded for the rest of the month. Is that clear?"

"Yes, sir," Kelley whimpered.

Bradford turned and slammed the door on his way out.

In the next room, Chris sat upright in his bed. His father's yelling had woken him. Hearing what he said to Kelly, he threw the covers back to go tell him that it was he who hit the tree. He jumped up but then saw his image in the mirror across the room. He was still in his clothes from last night, except now they were very wrinkled and his pants legs were stained in his own vomit. He heard his father slam Kelley's door. Too late, he thought. Chris flopped back onto the mattress, then pulled the bedspread over his head. "I screwed up again," he whispered.

Music: "Let's Get It Started" sung by Black Eyed Peas.
For Teenagers

Chapter 7

Week Two, Day One

Health is the greatest possession.
Contentment is the greatest treasure.
Confidence is the greatest friend.

--The Dhammapada

Chris and Kelley managed to avoid each other the rest of Sunday. Kelley stayed in her room, studying her AP Biology; Chris snuck out to the gym in the afternoon. Somehow they never met at the refrigerator.

When Chris walked into the kitchen on Monday morning, Kelley was already there, eating a banana. He sat, cowering, and took a deep breath.

"Kelley, I'm so sorry. I was an idiot. I admit it. I'll tell dad as soon as he comes in. I'm the one who should be grounded."

Kelley looked up at him. "No you won't," she said firmly. She handed him her cell phone. It was a text message from Sasha. Chris's eyes grew wide, and his mouth dropped open.

"Oh my god!" he said in a hushed whisper. "He broke his leg? Is this true?"

Kelley reached across the table and took the phone out of Chris's hand. She clicked to her photos and turned the cell back to Chris. He grabbed it from her in disbelief. There was a picture of Chase writhing in pain as he was rolled to an ambulance in the driveway of the Hazelton's house.

"What happened?" he exclaimed.

"It seems Chase had one too many beer bongs and fell backwards down the den stairs. After what I saw it do to you, I'm not surprised."

Chris hung his head and handed the phone back.

"I'm still telling dad, Kelley."

"No you're not, Chris. This is your chance. You'll be second string now. You'll get to play more."

"Kelley, I'm scared. What if I screw up?"

Kelley kicked him hard under the table.

"Ouch! What was that for?"

"Want a list?" she said grinning. "And that's for not believing in yourself. You'll be fine. Just try. I know how much this means to you."

Kelley looked into his sister's eyes. He pointed at his heart and then at hers.

Kelley smiled. "One more thing. You owe Luis, the gardener, a big 'thank you.' He's the one who carried you in and got the car out of the yard."

*   *   *   *   *

Mr. Doty was still writing on the board when the students entered English class. His students had developed the habit of looking at the board to see what quote would terrorize their evening. As they began to read, they quieted, some standing at their desks mouthing the words, others sitting and taking it in.

"Autobiography in Five Chapters"
by Portia Nelson

Chapter 1
I walk down the street.
There's a deep hole in the sidewalk.
I fall in.
I am lost... I am helpless.
It isn't my fault.
It takes forever to find my way out.

Chapter 2
I walk down the same street.
There's a deep hole in the sidewalk.
I pretend I don't see it.
I fall in, again.
I can't believe I'm in the same place, but it isn't my fault.
It still takes a long time to get out.

Chapter 3
I walk down the same street.
There's a deep hole in the sidewalk.
I see it there.
I fall in...it's a habit.
My eyes are open.
I know where I am.
It's my fault.
I get out immediately.

Chapter 4
I walk down the same street.
There is a deep hole in the sidewalk.
I walk around it.

Chapter 5
I walk down another street.

"Mr. Doty," called out Dina as the teacher walked to the front of the room. "Who's Portia Nelson?"

"Well, Dina, Portia was one of those wonderful people that too few people know about. She was a wonderful singer and songwriter during the height of the cabaret days in the 1950's. Marilyn Horne sang her song "Make a Rainbow" for President Bill Clinton's inauguration. Have you ever seen the movie 'The Sound of Music?'"

Dina nodded yes, as did most students in the room.

"Well, she was one of the singing nuns in that movie. This poem was given to me when I was going through some troubles in my life."

The class sat in silence. Many students see their teachers as simply just that, teachers. It never occurs to many of them that their teachers have their own personal goals and struggles.

"What did you do to get into trouble, Mr. Doty?" called out Malia, grinning. "Did you rob a bank?"

Mr. Doty smiled. "Now, I don't ask you whom you rob, do I? So don't ask me."

The class laughed. Mr. Doty turned and looked at the quote.

"For today's quote, I want you to be sure to ask an older family member. The quote speaks of coming to a turning point, and often one needs a bit of life experience to reach such a point. Feel free to call a grandparent or older relative if you like. Because it may take some extra time to talk with someone older, your response is not due until Wednesday."

"In keeping with the theme of turning points," he continued. "I'd like us to look at a short story by Tim O'Brien. Like our quote, it is autobiographical. Mr. O'Brien tells about deciding whether to go to fight in the

Vietnam War or run away to Canada—a huge turning point for him. Would you rather read silently or have me read it to you?"

"Aloud!" they yelled.

Mr. Doty knew this would be the answer. It never ceased to amaze him how most people love being read to regardless of their ages. The students were surprised by the ending. They talked about how hard it must have been to believe in your country but not believe in the war it was fighting. They were still talking excitedly when they filed out of the room fifty minutes later.

Kelley stayed behind at her seat at the end of class. She knew Mr. Doty had a planning period next. When the other students had left, she walked up to his desk.

"Mr. Doty, can I ask your advice about something?"

Mr. Doty smiled at her. "You may as long as you won't hold it against me for the rest of your life."

Kelley laughed.

"What's this about?"

"Well, you know we are all applying to colleges now, and my dad and I have a difference of opinion about where I should go and what I should study."

"What does he want?"

Kelley set her books down on a desk.

"Kelley, sit. I'll write you a note for your next class."

"Thanks," she said sitting. "My dad, well, he's a businessman, went to business school. He's determined that both Chris and I go to a school of his choosing and that we get MBAs."

Mr. Doty leaned back in his chair. "I gather you don't want to get a MBA?"

Kelley lowered her eyes. "No, I don't."

"What do you want to do, Kelley?"

She raised her head, her eyes sparkled. "Really, I mean, you wanna' know what I'd like to do?"

Mr. Doty laughed. "That was the question, I believe."

Kelley straightened up in her seat. "Okay, I've never told anybody this, but I want to major in medicine. Ideally, I want to work for Doctors Without Borders."

Mr. Doty clapped his hands. "That is very admirable, Kelley. Bravo!"

"But Mr. Doty, you don't know my dad. He doesn't take 'no' for an answer. I have to major in business. He's certain that's the only way I'll really be successful."

"I see," said the teacher. "Can I tell you about an interesting research study I read a while back? It was in a book by Mark Albion called <u>Making a Life, Making a Living</u>."

Kelley nodded yes and leaned forward in her seat.

"Mr. Albion quoted a study done of 1,500 business school graduates from 1960 to 1980. One group of these graduates said they wanted to make money first and *then* do what they really wanted. Of the 1,500 graduates, 93% were in this category. The other group said they wanted to follow their passions first, having faith that the money would come eventually.

"After twenty years there were 101 millionaires—1 from the first group and 100 from the second group."

"Wow!" exclaimed Kelley.

"Perhaps, Kelley, you can start with business and medicine."

"What do you mean?" she asked.

"Well, why don't you apply to colleges that have good business schools *and* good medical schools? Then you can decide later."

"Yea, I see what you mean. That will buy me some time. But Mr. Doty, I'm still worried that my dad will kill me if I don't go into business."

Mr. Doty smiled. "Kelley, as your English teacher, can I teach you some word etymology?"

"Sure," said Kelley, grinning.

"Well, the word *worry* comes from the Anglo-Saxon word that means *to choke* or *to strangle*. Worry cuts off the air of life."

Kelley sighed. "It sure does, doesn't it."

"There's an old saying, Kelley. Worry is an old man with bended head, carrying a load of feathers which he thinks are lead."

*   *   *   *   *

Maria was sliding the lasagna into the oven when she heard Mrs. Sparks' car drive up. A few minutes later she passed through the kitchen with some shopping bags. Maria yelled 'hello' over her shoulder as she sliced the French bread and began filling it with garlic butter. Allison mumbled a 'hello' and headed to the rear of the house.

Maria had been concerned about the Sparks family for some time now. Husband and wife had simply stopped being a couple about five years earlier. She didn't know what had happened, but they seemed to barely tolerate each other now. They had retreated into their own worlds—mortgages for the father and martinis for the mother. The last two months, however, had been especially dour. Mrs. Sparks had now stopped communicating with her children. Maria could see the hurt and confused looks on their faces, wondering if divorce was imminent and what might happen to them.

Children must feel so helpless when their parents are hurting, she thought.

Maria decided to do something special for Mrs. Sparks. She had just bought some black mission figs. She cut three of them in half and placed a slice of dry Pecorino Italian cheese on each piece, then headed back to the sun porch where she knew she'd find her.

Rather than sitting in her normal wicker chair facing the garden, Allison was sitting on the small sofa instead. A full martini sat on the end table. She looked up when Maria entered the room, her eyes puffy and red.

"Oh, Mrs. Sparks, what is wrong?" sighed Maria as she walked over and set the plate of figs down.

"Oh, I was reading something, and it made me sad," she said, wiping her eyes with a Kleenex.

"What are you reading, Mrs. Sparks?"

Allison handed the open book to Maria. She looked down and read aloud.

"You become. It takes a long time. That's why it doesn't often happen to people who break easily, or have sharp edges, or who have to be carefully kept. Generally, by the time you are Real, most of your hair has been loved off, and your eyes drop out and you get loose in the joints and very shabby. But these things don't matter at all, because once you are Real you can't be ugly, except to people who don't understand."

Maria turned the cover over and read the title, "The Velveteen Rabbit by Margery Williams."

"Mrs. Sparks, why are you worried about getting ugly and shabby," she said, looking back down at Allison.

Allison's bottom lip trembled. She started to answer but then hunched over in a fetal position, weeping. Maria sat down next to her and lifted her up to a sitting position. She cradled her as a mother does a child, wrapping her big arms around her. Maria held her head close to her bosom, and Allison sobbed and sobbed.

When the tears had finally subsided, Maria pulled back. Taking Allison's chin, she turned her head to face hers.

"Mrs. Sparks, enough already," she said firmly. "You tell me right now what is eating at you. I will not let you sit in despair like this."

Allison used her sleeve to wipe her eyes. "Oh, Maria. I can't."

"Oh yes you can. And you will!"

Sometimes the most painful thing is an act of kindness. Mrs. Sparks talked for a solid hour. Maria never let her go.

Music: "Everybody Is A Star" by Sly and the Family Stone.
For Mr. Doty and all Teachers

Chapter 8

Week Two, Day Two

Argue for your limitations
and sure enough
they're yours.

--Illusions
Richard Bach

The tires of a large truck from the local nursery ground through the gravel of the Sparks' driveway at seven a.m. Tuesday morning. Bradford heard the truck and walked outside to review what was going on. The truck looked like it was carrying a rain forest—everything from tall bamboo to Japanese dwarf red maples to Mondo grass. Jesus, he thought. This is going to cost me a bundle.

The gardener was helping the driver swing around in order to back up to the yard. He waved the truck backwards to the beep-beep of the reverse signal on the truck. Bradford strode past him out to his tree. To his relief he could see that Kelley had only knocked a small chip out of it.

"Mr. Sparks, will you be helping us do some planting today?" Bradford turned around, looking down at the gardener who had crept up on him.

"What's your name?" he asked crossly.

"Luis."

"Well, Luis, I have no intention of helping you dig holes. That's what I'm paying you for. I have my own fields to tend."

Luis's eyes brightened. "If I may ask, sir, what is your field?"

Bradford pulled his Blackberry from his coat pocket and stared at it for a moment, then looked at Luis. "Business, mortgages specifically." He slipped the Blackberry back inside his coat. "A field on which real men find their worth. Not on an old prairie being made into a garden."

Luis nodded. "Yes, I'm sure our fields seem very different. What worth are you finding then, if you don't mind me asking?"

"Worth? Well, money of course. And lots of it in the last few years," Bradford answered smugly. "How do you think I paid for this mansion, these cars?" he said waving his long arm towards the house. "And I'm looking to make lots more. We may be having a little problem with a few foreclosures right now, but that's normal. Business is always a battle. I fully intend to stay ahead of my adversaries."

"Adversaries?" asked Luis.

Bradford kicked at the dirt. "Hell yes, adversaries. This *is* capitalism, you know. And in capitalism someone always wins and someone loses. It's always a battle. Other businesses battle for your clients. Your own colleagues battle for your position. Those above you undermine you by stealing the credit for what you've achieved." He glanced towards the house. "Hell, even people you live with don't appreciate what you've given them. They don't have a clue how hard you work to turn useless prairies like this into housing developments that make money."

"It sounds as if everyone is against you, Mr. Sparks."

Bradford turned to the man. "Listen, I don't need condescension from a gardener. Jesus, look at you," he said, pointing to Luis's dirt-covered jeans. "You still make a living working in dirt."

Luis smiled. "It sounds like we both do."

Bradford stared into his large brown eyes. "Just pull the damn weeds."

*   *   *   *   *

Chris had been watching from the kitchen window, waiting for his dad to leave. He certainly didn't look happy when he walked away from the gardener. Damn, he thought. Now he's pissed off the guy, and I've got to apologize to him.

When he heard his dad's SUV pull away, he walked out to the back yard. Luis was walking backwards, dragging a potted eight-foot tall bamboo towards the back fence. Chris had never seen bamboo like this. The stalks were a bright yellow with green rings on them. The leaves on the bamboo made a swishing sound as Luis pulled it.

"Excuse me!" called out Chris.

Luis kept moving, pulling the large pot but smiling at Chris.

Chris followed him to the back until the gardener had placed the pot. He stepped back, considering its position.

Chris also studied the pot standing against the redwood fence. "Hey, like it's none of my business, but do you think the plant looks good in that black plastic container?"

90

Luis looked at the boy, then at the potted bamboo. "Hmm, well, what would you suggest?"

Chris turned to the gardener. "Well, why don't you take the bamboo out of the pots and plant them so they look more natural?"

Luis placed his hand on his chin for a few seconds and appeared to be thinking.

"I see your point. You know, I think you have a very good idea. But these pots are made of thick plastic," Luis said kicking at the heavy pot. "Do you think we can get the plants out of them? I only have a small box cutter and . . ."

"Give it here," said Chris confidently. "I'll have that bamboo free in a flash."

Luis reached in his back pocket and handed him the cutter. Chris walked straight to the potted plant.

"Well, if you don't mind then, I'll go drag another bamboo back here while you set this one free."

The plastic pot was much thicker than Chris had imagined. He tried to pull the cutter through the plastic from top to bottom, but he couldn't get a good grasp on it. Finally, he laid the plant on its side so that he could straddle it and slice the plastic with the full force of his throwing arm. After three slices, he freed the bamboo.

Lifting the plant upright, he turned to show Luis. The gardener had brought another bamboo up to the fence and was walking back for a third. Chris glanced at the new plant, then looked at his watch. He didn't have to leave for school for thirty minutes. Oh well, he thought, I owe this guy anyway.

Chris had just freed his fourth bamboo when he remembered why he had come out to the garden in the first place. When Luis dragged the fifth pot up, he turned to him.

91

"Hey, uh, Luis, look, I came out here to apologize for the other night."

Luis straightened up from the pot he'd been pulling.

"Well," said Luis. "I'm glad that's why you came. I was afraid you were going to ask me for driving lessons."

Chris laughed. "Yea, my parking is a little rusty, isn't it?"

"Not as rusty as your reverse," said Luis, laughing. "May I ask you a question?"

"Sure," said Chris, setting down the cutter and wiping his brow.

"Why did you drink so much?"

Chris looked down at his shoes. "Well, it's fun, ya know. It's what the older guys do. I'm just trying to keep up."

"You didn't look like you were having a lot of fun Friday night?"

"No, I guess not." He paused for a few seconds. "Look, it's important to be accepted. Guys drink. It's cool. It's what we do," he said shrugging his shoulders.

Chris felt a small pain in his right arm from cutting the thick plastic. He began rubbing it.

"Did you hurt yourself?"

"No, just pulled a muscle. I just need to be careful. I'm on the football team, a quarterback," he said, throwing his shoulders back. "Well, actually I'm the third-string quarterback. But our first-string broke his leg this weekend, so now I'm the second."

Luis took a seat on the ground. "This sounds like a violent game!"

"Oh, well, he didn't break his leg in a game. He fell down the stairs at the party I was at the other night. He was pretty drunk."

"Oh, doing what guys do," said Luis smiling.

Chris looked at the gardener. "Look, I'm sorry I got drunk and wrecked the car, but don't criticize the guys on the team. Chase is a great quarterback. Much more than I'll ever be. He's a natural. So, he got drunk and broke his leg. Stuff happens. Anyway, Coach is putting the second-string quarterback in full time. It really doesn't affect me."

"How does it not affect you?" asked the gardener.

Chris shrugged his shoulders. "Look, I'm just not that good. I do what I can. They play me a little when we run the score up. That's all. I'm just not a natural like Chase."

Luis stared up at the tall boy, who dug the toe of his tennis shoe into the loose dirt. "Chris, have you ever heard of a flea circus?" asked Luis.

Chris's eyes grew wide.

"Yea, I guess so. I mean, isn't it a miniature circus where the fleas jump around in a box or something? They used to have them at fairs."

"Exactly. Now, have you ever wondered why the fleas don't just jump out of the box and escape?"

"They must be stupid, I guess. I don't know. Why?"

"Well, when the flea trainer first gets the fleas, he puts a lid on the box. At first the fleas jump up to the top trying to get out, but they keep hitting their heads on the lid. After a while though, something curious happens. The fleas get tired of hitting their heads so they jump lower. At this point the trainer takes the lid off the box, but now the fleas have convinced themselves of their limitations, so they never try to jump any higher."

Chris looked over at the garage. Kelley was there, waiting for him to take her to school. He turned back to Luis. "So, you're telling me I should jump higher?"

Luis smiled. "I'm just saying that if you do, be prepared to take a few hits."

*   *   *   *   *

Allison made her entrance into the garden at three in the afternoon. She felt her ensemble was spot on. The white overalls from Nordstrom's were lightly adorned with yellow daisies. Her yellow blouse from Saks matched the color of the flowers perfectly. The gloves from Restoration Hardware were also yellow with a green liner on the palms for better gripping. She had initially chosen some spectacular Jimmy Choo sandals for footwear, but remembering that this was a garden, not a garden party, she settled with a pair that was less patrician, more plebian. To top off the outfit, she had picked out a white floppy hat with a yellow band.

The gardener was all the way in the far back of the yard, placing and planting the tall Alphonse Carr bamboo. Allison marveled at how the bamboo swayed in the wind, producing a light swishing sound that softened the look and feel of the stark redwood fence.

"Hello, Luis. I'm ready!" she called out as she approached.

Luis was on his knees, but immediately stood up and turned.

"My goodness, Mrs. Sparks! You do look nice!" he exclaimed.

Allison smiled. A compliment from a man. It had been a while, she realized.

"Now, Mrs. Sparks, you do know that you will be working in dirt, right?" said Luis candidly.

Allison's expression fell. "Well, uh, yes, of course. But I thought you would be doing most of the dirty work. I imagined I could help out with other tasks in the garden."

Luis smiled. "I'm afraid that when one tends a garden, one gets dirty, but the rewards are abundant. Now, how do you like the placement of the bamboo so far?"

Allison looked down the length of the fence and scanned the twelve yellow and green plants swaying in the wind. "It's beautiful, Luis."

Luis smiled broadly. "I'm so glad you like it. I have two more of these to get into the ground, and I thought we'd put the Mondo grass around the edges of the patio. Would you please bring the pots up to the patio and place them about four inches apart? After that, you'll need to dig six inch holes for each, pour in some compost from the large bag over there, then drop the plants in. There's a trowel for you to work with. I'll be over to help you as soon as I finish the bamboo."

Allison stared at him in disbelief. Luis took in her reaction.

"Oh, I see," said Luis quickly. "I'm assuming too much, aren't I? Sorry. Follow me, please, Mrs. Sparks."

Allison followed the little man towards the house, glad that he had obviously come to his senses and reconsidered her role. Perhaps he would have her call out planting suggestions from a lawn chair. He stopped, however, beside a large group of small pots, each filled with a rich green grass that sprayed upwards like a water splash.

"*This* is the Mondo grass, Mrs. Sparks," Luis said pointing at the pots. He then turned and walked back to the fence, picked up a shovel and began digging a large hole for another bamboo.

*   *   *   *   *

Kelley came home directly from school. Being grounded wasn't so horrible, she thought. She could finally catch up on her AP reading in three classes.

"Hey, Maria. What's for dinner tonight?" she called out as she entered the kitchen from the garage.

Maria was facing the counter. Kelley could see a knife in her right hand. She went up behind her and wrapped her arms around Maria, looking over her shoulder. An unpeeled onion sat in front of her on a cutting board. Suddenly Maria sniffed.

"Maria?" said Kelley, confused. Maria stood still. Kelley dropped her arms and moved to the counter where she could see her. Tear tracks lined her dark brown face.

"Maria, what's wrong?"

Maria wiped her left cheek with her sleeve. "Nothing, honey." She began to peel the onion.

Kelley had rarely seen Maria sad. She didn't know how to respond.

"Well, that must be an awfully strong onion if you're crying before you slice it," she said, trying to make her laugh.

Maria stopped peeling and took a deep breath. "Sorry, *mija*. I was just thinking about stuff. How was school today?"

Kelley felt something was wrong, but she was afraid to push any further. She was glad to change the subject.

"Oh, everybody was talking about Chase breaking his leg. We heard the coaches were really mad. The whole team is bummed. And evidently his dad is furious. He's worried Chase may have blown his chance for a scholarship."

She reached for a bit of sliced celery but immediately got her hand slapped.

"Hey, Maria, I need your help," she said withdrawing her stinging hand. "My English teacher gave us this quote about turning points, and I have to get a reaction from someone who's, uh, uh, . . ."

Maria smiled. "Older?"

Kelley laughed. "Yea, well as he says, 'someone with more life experience.' Would you look at this for a second?"

She pulled the poem out of her backpack and laid it on the counter. Maria read it slowly, then picked it up and handed it back to Kelley. A tear ran down her cheek.

"Kelley, I think you should ask your mother about this."

Kelley looked surprised. "Why her?"

"Because your mother is a strong person and she has lots to share. You need to learn more about her life. Now go ask her," said Maria firmly, starting to peel the onion.

"Okay, okay. Where is she? Is she in the sunroom already?"

Maria looked up and smiled. "Well, believe it or not, you'll find her digging in the garden."

Kelley couldn't believe her eyes as she walked on the flag stone path across the yard. All she could see was her mother's white rump until she straightened up with a large bag in her arms. Dirt was falling out of the bag onto her mother's feet.

"Mom?"

Allison turned around. The white overalls were now dark brown. Smudges of dirt streaked her face and arms and a weed hung from her hair. As Kelley approached, she gasped to see her mother's pedicured toes and sandals caked in mud. With mouth hanging open, she looked up into her mother's broad smile.

"Hello, dear!" Allison exclaimed brightly.

"Mother, *what* are you doing?" Kelley exclaimed.

Allison laughed. "Why, dear, this is called gardening. You should try it sometime. It's quite exhilarating."

Kelley looked down at her mom's work. The ragged edge of the flag stone patio had now been softened with clumps of beautiful green grass spaced precisely around its edge.

"Did you do this?" asked Kelley.

"Yes, of course, dear," said Allison smugly. "Your mother has many talents. Now, Luis wants me to finish with these before dinner, and I have six more to put in, so what is it you want?"

Kelley looked up from the plants. "Well, I hate to bother you, but my English teacher wants me to ask a family member to respond to a poem. It's called 'An Autobiography in Five Chapters.'"

Allison's right eyebrow rose. "Honey, I don't have time to read five chapters right now."

"No, mom, it's very short. It's only one page. Would you at least give it a quick look?" Kelley asked as she pulled the quote out.

Allison pulled off her dirty glove and held out her hand for the paper. She read quietly for a moment. The smile disappeared from her face. Oh no, not again, thought Kelley. What is it with this poem?

Allison took a deep breath, straightened up her shoulders and looked her daughter in the eye. "Honey, I think I'm about ready to walk down a different street. Let's go sit down. I want to talk to you."

**Music: "Follow Me" sung by Peter, Paul and Mary.
For Allison and Kelley**

Chapter 9

Week Two, Day Three

When you meet anyone, remember it is a holy encounter.
As you see him you will see yourself.
As you treat him you will treat yourself.
As you think of him you will think of yourself.
Never forget this, for in him you will find yourself
or lose yourself.

--A Course of Miracles

Kelley and Allison had talked for most of the evening. There had been lots of tears, lots of hugs, but mostly, and finally, understanding and empathy.

Two months earlier Allison had found a lump on her right breast. She simply wasn't able to deal with it and she didn't know whom to turn to. She came to the horrible realization that she didn't feel comfortable sharing the news with a single one of her society friends. She and her husband had quit sharing intimacies years earlier. Feeling alone and lost, she kept her terror to herself. Finally, a month ago she gathered the courage to get a mammogram. Her worst fears were confirmed—breast cancer.

Her depression became so great that she began to self-destruct, using alcohol to numb the pain. As Kelley listened, she began to understand her mother's withdrawal into a martini. But the knowledge was a lot for a high school senior to deal with. She and Maria were the only people outside of medicine who knew anything.

Gathering her courage, she told her mother they would have to make some decisions, together.

Sitting alone at the breakfast table on Wednesday, she reviewed the promises she and her mother made the night before. Kelley agreed to keep the news to herself for now. She also agreed that if she became too frightened, she would talk to Maria or a school counselor. Allison begged her not to tell her school friends, and Kelley understood why. High school girls rarely kept secrets. Her mother was to start chemo on Monday, so as a trade off, Kelley made her promise to tell dad before the end of the weekend. Both agreed not to tell Chris just yet.

"Hey Kelley Koo Koo! Why you look so blue?" sang Chris as he bounded into the kitchen.

Kelley looked up at her brother and whispered across the table as he sat down. "Hey, were you throwing up in the bathroom this morning?"

Chris avoided her gaze. "Yea, just a little morning sickness. I'm pregnant," he said trying to make a joke.

"No really, Chris. What is it?"

Chris held up his two hands and shook them as if they were trembling.

"Nerves again?" asked Kelley sympathetically.

"Yea, it's this quarterback thing. I was safe before as number three, but now they may actually play me. What if the other guy gets hurt?"

"Look, Chris . . ."

She stopped when she heard her father's footsteps. Bradford came through the doorway.

"Did you come home right after school, young lady?" he asked gruffly, setting his briefcase in his chair.

"Yes, sir," mumbled Kelley.

"Good, be sure you do the same for the next thirteen days."

"Breakfast this morning?" asked Maria, coming around the corner with a plate of scrambled eggs and bacon for Kelley.

"No, Maria, I can't," he said, checking his Blackberry. "This damn foreclosure business seems to be spreading. I need to get to the office."

He looked at Maria. "I just don't get these stupid people. We bend over backwards to get them a house, and then they freak out because their interest rate goes up a little. Jeez! They're just frightened sheep."

Bradford reached across the table and took a piece of toast out of the toaster. He snatched his briefcase out of the chair and headed out into the garage. Maria set the breakfast plate in front of Kelley.

"Maria, I think I'm gonna' skip breakfast today," said Kelley, staring at the yellow eggs.

Chris reached over and stole her plate. "Works for me! My stomach feels like it's completely empty!" he said, winking at Kelley.

Maria moved behind Chris's chair. "Kelley, I'll let you pass today," she said with a knowing nod. "But we're going to need you strong and healthy, right?"

Kelley nodded, then turned to Chris. "Hey, bud. I'm gonna' catch the bus today, so you go on without me, okay?"

Chris was shoving in a mouthful of eggs. "Sure," he mumbled.

Kelley got up from the table and climbed the stairs to her mother's room. The door was still closed. She quietly opened it and looked in. Allison was curled in a fetal position in the bed, her arms wrapped around a pillow. The early morning light fell on her mother's pallid face. She must be so frightened, she thought.

Quietly shutting the door, Kelley went to her room and turned on her computer. "My mother is not going to fight this alone," she whispered.

Bringing up Google, she typed in *Breast Cancer Support Groups* and began searching. She never heard the school bus stop outside, nor did she hear Maria look in on her and then quietly close her door.

On the way to his car, Bradford had stopped to survey the progress in the garden. The gardener was digging a hole beside a potted Japanese red maple. Bradford watched the man work for a few minutes. The little guy certainly is focused, he thought. He checked his watch, spun around and retreated to his car. Sticking his key in the ignition, he looked out through the windshield only to see a piece of paper stuck under the wiper. He turned on the wipers, trying to throw it off, but it just waved at him back and forth, back and forth. Damn these illegals, he thought. They can't even read the 'No Solicitors' sign at the end of the driveway.

Cursing, he unbuckled his seatbelt and climbed out of the car, grabbing the note. As he began to crumple it up, he caught a glimpse of his name on the front. Jumping back into the car, he buckled his seatbelt, straightened out the paper, and read softly to himself.

"Mr. Bradford, 'All kinds of men visit the prairie. Some see only the danger. Some see only ugliness. Some seek victims to satisfy their own pleasures there. Some are timid, some fearless, some frightened, but all people who visit this place share one important thing. They share their aloneness. We face only ourselves on the prairie. We can discover ourselves there, or we can simply run with the animals of the prairie, blindly and at nature's whims. The prairie, my children, is life.'

from <u>Seven Arrows</u> by Hyemeyohsts Storm"

*   *   *   *   *

Around ten in the morning Allison walked into the kitchen as Maria was cleaning up.

"Ah, Mrs. Sparks, there you are. Have a seat. I made you a yogurt parfait with fresh fruit and granola."

Allison started to speak but Maria cut her off. "Nope! I will not hear a word. You need your strength now more than ever. *Sientate!*"

Obediently Allison sat down. She watched Luis working in the garden.

"So, what are your plans for today?" asked Maria.

Allison dug her spoon into the parfait glass. "I believe I have some gardening to do."

"*Bueno!*" said Maria.

After breakfast, Allison went into the mudroom by the garage and changed into her overalls. Much to her delight, Maria had cleaned them. She walked out into the sunlight of the garden, took a deep breath, and headed over to Luis who was working beside a red maple. He had just planted one by the fence on the left. He turned when he heard her coming.

"Ah, Mrs. Sparks. I was worried about you. I saw that you had not punched the time clock at eight this morning. I was afraid I worked you too hard yesterday."

Allison laughed. "No, Luis, you didn't work me too hard. I'm ready to go again. I was just waiting for my husband to get out of the house," she said, pulling on her gloves.

Luis punched the tip of the shovel into the dirt. "Mrs. Sparks, excuse me for asking, but your husband seems like an angry man. Why is that?"

Allison looked away, silent.

"I'm sorry, Mrs. Sparks. That is none of . . ."

"No, no, it's fine, Luis. My husband *is* an angry man, and I guess I am partly to blame. We haven't gotten along for quite a while, and I'll admit sometimes I enjoy making him miserable."

She stepped over to the maple and began to caress the fragile red leaves. "It's odd, Luis, how things can deteriorate to such an extent and yet you don't realize how bad they are getting as it happens. We started out great the first few years, but the kids came and . . ." She paused. "No, I'm not going to blame it on the kids. They have been great. I don't know, somehow we went from loving each other, to taking each other for granted, and now there are times I'm sure we loathe each other. We probably would have divorced if it weren't for the kids, and who knows, we still might. There doesn't seem to be any hope that we'll ever turn our marriage around."

Luis took his gloves off. "Mrs. Sparks, may I offer a medieval perspective."

Allison raised her right eyebrow. "A perspective from the Dark Ages? Somehow that sounds appropriate right now."

"Well, I learned it from Joseph Campbell, who was a wonderful scholar who taught at Sarah Lawrence College. He was one of those rare people who seemed to be a walking encyclopedia. He became an expert on spirituality and folklore. In his lectures, he told ancient stories, myths, and legends from many cultures and from many time periods to show how similar man's hopes and fears are. Now, I'm sure you've watched the game show *Wheel of Fortune*?"

Allison nodded.

"Well, the wheel of fortune was a favorite image in the Middle Ages. Most people saw their lives as revolving around the rim of the wheel. At the top, everything is going great. But eventually the wheel turns and things go sour. However, over time, the wheel keeps turning and things get better.

"Joseph Campbell says this is the sense with the marriage vow. You take your partner going up and going down, in sickness and in health, in poverty and in wealth."

Allison looked at Luis with a grin. "Didn't they used to break people on the wheel?" she asked.

Luis laughed. "Yes, they did."

"So you're saying that life is always ups and downs and to just live with it?"

"Well, that is one choice."

"And the other?" she inquired, now genuinely interested.

"Well, you can choose to live on the rim, or you can live on the hub. You see, when two people find each other's center, they find the hub. And it is from this space they can watch the drama of the world turn and yet feel bliss in their love and security with each other."

Allison looked at her mud-caked sandals. "I'm afraid my husband and I have lost our centers."

She looked up at Luis, into his sparkling brown eyes.

"You haven't lost them, Mrs. Sparks. You just haven't chosen to look for them in a while."

*   *   *   *   *

Bradford had gotten to the office with high hopes. The market actually rallied Tuesday. He was hoping that the Asian markets had followed their lead over night. The desperate quietness of the office let him know otherwise. At every cubicle heads stared silently into blue-green screens, taking in the free fall of the credit system.

As he sat down, he saw that he had seven messages on his answering machine. Might as well deal with these first, he thought. Picking up the receiver, he dialed in his voicemail and heard a priority message. It was from the company president in the head office back east. Bradford listened.

"As you all know, the credit market is going through a turbulent time. For these reasons, we want all regional offices to take a more conservative approach in the coming weeks. Please notify your staff that as of this coming Friday, we will no longer issue any subprime mortgages. Regional managers are to continue to sell any existing signed mortgages to banks that still accept them. It is our belief that the large investment banks will continue to bundle these mortgages into other securities until the end of the month. Regrettably, should this crisis continue, we will naturally need to begin making layoffs to contain costs. Please begin to formulate a list of those whom you can lay off beginning with the sales assistants and then sales personnel. It is also possible that regions with an excessive number of foreclosures will have to close their offices sometime in the future. Hopefully this crisis will pass, and we can get back to business as normal. Have a great day."

He had no sooner hung up the phone than it rang again.

"All American Mortgage. This is Bradford. How can I put you in a, uh, ... How can I help you?"

"Mr. Bradford. I'm so glad to speak to you. This is Mrs. Kowalski. Do you remember me?"

"Of course I do, Mrs. Kowalksi. How are you?" he replied, trying to stall for time as he thumbed through the mortgages sitting on his desk, looking for her name.

"Well, Mr. Bradford, I'm very concerned. You know I watch the evening news every night, and all they are talking about are these foreclosures."

Bradford found her file. "Now Mrs. Kowalski, don't let the news confuse you. The market always goes up and down. But remember, over the long term it eventually gains. This market is only affecting interest rates right now, and your money is not in the market, is it?"

There was a moment of silence on the phone. "No, I guess not," replied Mrs. Kowalski timidly.

"Exactly Mrs. Kowalski, and as you well know, there is no safer place to have your money than in a home, right?"

"Well, I guess so. It's just that this is all the money I have left from my husband's retirement. I'm a little nervous about having signed that contract last week."

"Mrs. Kowalski, now don't you worry. I promise I'll look after you."

"Really?" she said, her voice brightening.

"Really," Bradford said reassuringly. "Now, is there anything else?"

"No, I guess not."

"Well, goodbye then Mrs. Kowalski."

"Bye bye," she said and hung up.

Bradford hung up the phone, threw the signed mortgage back on the stack to be sent out Friday, and cradled his aching head in his hands.

Music: "Never Comes the Day" sung by The Moody Blues.
For Bradford

Chapter 10

Week Two, Day Four

You are the way and the wayfarers
And when one of you falls down
he falls for those behind him,
a caution against the stumbling stone.
Ay, and he falls for those ahead of him,
who though faster and surer of foot,
yet removed not the stumbling stone.

--The Prophet
Kahlil Gibran

Kelley's cell rang as she stared out the school bus window. It was Sasha.

"Hey girl, what's up?" rang Sasha's voice.

"I'm riding the bus, counting the stops."

"Why didn't you come with your brother?"

"He wanted to get to school early. He's been studying football plays with the other quarterback every morning since Chase got hurt."

"Hey, did you do your AP Biology homework?" asked Sasha.

"And why would you be asking? What exactly were you doing last night?" replied Kelley impishly.

"I was doing AP Math. She promised a quiz today, and I am like way behind. And no, I was not doing it while ordering a smoothie from Carlos."

Kelley laughed. "Okay, I'll help you with Biology but you gotta' help me with today's English quote."

"Jeez! Like is Doty still assigning those things?"

"Yea, hey, we're pulling into the school now. See ya in the library in ten."

Ten minutes later Kelley was at their usual table, waiting. Suddenly her phone vibrated. It was a text message from Sasha.

"Hey, can't meet now. Peyton wants to talk. **ttyl**."

Kelley leaned back in her seat. She had finished all her homework but the English quote. Hmm, she thought. Who can help me?

Across the room she spied Ms. O'Neal, the librarian. She had only been at the school for two years but had already transformed the atmosphere of the library. Checking out books from the old librarian was like checking out the royal jewels from the Tower of London. A cold pallor followed the lady around the room, and most students only went there to sleep.

The first thing Ms. O'Neal did was to order tons of adolescent novels, especially graphic novels, which are a new version of comic books but with much more sophisticated art. The circulation of the library doubled. Boys especially sat transfixed at tables, pouring over action-packed stories and beautiful illustrations. Ms. O'Neal had now hung tablets on the graphic novel bookshelves so students could add their names to Waiting Lists for particular books.

Kelley waited until Ms. O'Neal walked past. "Ms. O'Neal, may I ask you a question?"

The short lady turned, smiling, her owl like eyes sparkling.

"Yes, of course, Kelley. How can I help you?"

"Well, Mr. Doty wants us to ask older people what they think of certain quotes."

Ms. O'Neal's eyebrows rose. "He does, does he. Hmmm. So I am your older person for today?"

Kelley laughed. "Do you mind?"

"No, of course not. Let's see what the quote is."

Kelley turned the paper so that the librarian could read it.

"Ah, Kahlil Gibran. Nice!"

"You know this guy!" asked Kelley.

"Well, I'm old, my dear, but I'm not *that* old. Let's step over to the computer and find out about Mr. Gibran."

Kelley sat down and immediately typed in Kahlil Gibran's name in the Google search bar. A list of web sites appeared, and she moved her cursor over to Wikipedia. Ms. O'Neal placed her hand on Kelley's.

"Why don't we start with a more reliable site first? How about this one?" she said, pointing to another site on the list.

Kelley began reading. "Wow, he lived a long time ago—born in 1883. And he was an Arab, from Lebanon!"

Kelley read on. "It says his parents split up. He, his mom, and his sisters moved to South Boston. They were poor; she sewed lace for a living. Oh man, he lost his two sisters and his half brother within one year. Let's see, he was also an artist and illustrated his own books. He was well known, but became famous again in the counterculture of the 1960's. Cool. 'Let the Sun Shine In,'" sang Kelley.

Ms. O'Neal laughed. "I *am* old enough to know that one."

"And he died of cancer." Kelley grew silent at this.

Ms. O'Neal leaned in. "So Kelley, what do you think his quote means?"

Kelley looked up. "Hey, I'm supposed to ask you that," she said smiling.

Ms. O'Neal smiled and pulled out a chair to sit beside her. "Let me read it again." She read aloud.

You are the way and the wayfarers
And when one of you falls down
he falls for those behind him,
a caution against the stumbling stone.
Ay, and he falls for those ahead of him,
who though faster and surer of foot,
yet removed not the stumbling stone.

--The Prophet
Kahlil Gibran

"Well," she said, after a moment. Since we process everything through our own experience, to me this is a statement about teachers and librarians, of course."

Kelley gave Ms. O'Neal a curious look. "How?"

"Well, teachers are here to show students a way, but we are on our own journey too. When we see a student stumble, it lets us know where other students may have problems, so it warns of possible stumbling blocks. And when we see students move quickly ahead, it shows us possible paths we might take to help all of our students. That's especially true today, when many of you use technology in ways we teachers never dreamed.

"But there's more to this, I think. Maybe this quote tells us that life is a journey, not a race. In a race, one runs with only one motive, to beat the others. On a journey, one stops and shares his or her experiences with others, making sure they see the beauty and the wonder of life. For me, Kelley, that is exactly what great teachers, and librarians, do."

*　　*　　*　　*　　*

Bradford pulled onto the freeway and into the slow-moving right lane. He rode in silence, lost in thought. How could all this have happened? "I did everything right," he murmured. A small red Mini-Cooper pulled up along side of him, passing. The driver yelled something and gave him the finger. Bradford stared back, numb.

When he got home, he walked straight back to his office. He had to try to salvage something. There had to be a way out of this mess. He sat behind his desk and pulled out the bottom file drawer that contained all of the family financial papers. "Okay," he said. "Let's just take stock of what we owe. Then I can make some decisions."

He studied his own mortgage first. It was a thirty-year fixed at a good rate. If he could keep some semblance of income coming in, he would be able to keep the house. Property taxes and home insurance would be difficult to meet. Allison would need to be put on a strict budget, as would the kids. Jeez, the kids, he realized. Say goodbye to the top MBA schools. Kelley's college fund would get her through two years at least at a state school. They had barely put away anything for Chris's education.

"Let's check the other monthly expenses," he said to himself. Rummaging through the folder he found his car payments for three of the four cars! Okay, the kids would have to share one, and he'd sell the Escalade and get something more fuel-efficient. Next he found the four cell phone bills, the cable, electricity and gas, garbage pick up, and yard service. Well, that was easy to fix. The gardener would be gone tomorrow.

Beneath these statements were the credit card bills. He'd have to consolidate the cards down to one or

113

two with the lowest interest rates. He looked over the long statements. They had been spending with abandon, all of them. So here is all our happiness, he thought.

Bradford closed the folders and buried his head in his hands. "And what if the worst happens," he mumbled. "What if they close the office and fire me? What will we do for health insurance, for food? How will we pay Maria?"

He felt a hollow feeling in his throat—a feeling he hadn't felt in years. The same feeling he had at sixteen when he walked out on his dad, an abusive alcoholic, swearing he'd make something of himself. He knew this feeling. It was profound fear. What if he screwed up?

A knock at his office door brought him out of his daze. "What is it?" he yelled.

"Dad, it's Chris. Can I talk to you a second?"

What does the kid want now, he thought. He quickly put the financial papers back in the drawer. "Yea, come in."

Chris walked in timidly. He was wearing his blue and gold football jersey.

"Why do you have that thing on?" asked Bradford, pointing at his shirt.

"Oh, we had a pep rally at school today for the game tomorrow," Chris said, standing in front of his dad's large desk.

"So what do you want, son? I'm kind of busy."

Chris looked down at his shoes. "Dad, I kind of wanted to talk to you about the game."

"Look," Bradford interrupted. "If it's about me coming . . ."

"No, dad. It's not that. I think I'd rather you weren't there anyway."

This surprised Bradford. "Really! Why is that?"

114

"Well, it's kind of hard to talk about."

"Just spit it out, son."

Chris paused, obviously trying to gather his strength. "Dad, I'm really scared. The first string quarterback broke his leg, so they may play me. I mean, play me a lot more than normal. Jeez, dad, I'm not sure I can do it. I mean, what if I screw up?" He reached up with his sleeve and wiped his right eye.

For the first time in years, Bradford saw his son. He saw him because he finally heard him. And he finally heard him because he knew exactly what he was feeling. He cleared his throat.

"Hey buddy, sit down a moment."

Chris sat down in the large leather chair across from his dad. He still wouldn't look his father in the eye.

"Look, fear is natural. It's a way for your body to get prepared to do something extraordinary. You just can't let it overwhelm you. Understand?"

Chris nodded, staring down into his hands. Bradford didn't feel as if he was getting through. He glanced down at his desk and saw the Post-Its he kept stuck to the surface.

"Chris, when I get frightened . . ."

Chris looked up, eyes wide. "You get frightened?"

Bradford laughed. "Son, everyone gets frightened. But when I do, I remember Abraham Lincoln. You know why?"

Chris shook his head no.

"Lincoln ran for public office seven times and failed and he still became one of our greatest presidents. I keep this quote on my desk to remind me of his courage."

Bradford pulled up the Post-It and handed it to Chris.

115

Chris read it aloud. "Always bear in mind that your own resolution to succeed is more important than any one thing."

Chris looked up at his father. "So, if I just decide to succeed, that's supposed to get me through? What if I screw up anyway?"

Bradford smiled. "Well, son, in business you always have a backup plan. That's why I keep this second Post-It here too."

He pulled up another Post-It from the desk and handed it to Chris.

Chris read aloud again. "To fear the worst oft cures the worst. William Shakespeare." He looked at his dad, confused.

"Son, go ahead and play out the scenario in your mind that you screw up. Then ask yourself, is it really the end of the world? Won't life go on? Won't you have other chances? And will any of this matter thirty years from now? In other words, look past the failure and realize there's so much more life to be lived."

Chris stared back down at his lap. "Dad, that's easy for you to say. You never screw up."

Bradford fell back into his seat. At that moment he realized how little he and his son knew about each other. "Bud, listen, I screw up. Everybody's does."

Still staring down, Chris said, "Yea, like when?"

Bradford paused, took in a breath. "Like right now."

Chris's head shot up. "What do you mean?"

"Son, I gather you've been hearing about the stock market losses over the last few weeks."

Chris nodded yes.

"Well, the cause of the drop is the mortgage business. We've been writing too many loans that people can't really pay. Now the banks want their money, and there isn't any."

"What's going to happen, dad?"

"I don't know. I think it's going to get very bad."

"Are we in trouble?" asked Chris, clearly concerned.

Bradford let out a small chuckle. "Well, let's just say I was in here going through my backup plan. I think we're going to get hit by this, son. We're definitely going to have to cut back on our spending."

There was silence for a moment.

"I'm sorry, dad."

Bradford looked his son in the eyes. "Son, it's not your fault. I'm the one who screwed up."

"No, dad. I'm sorry I came in here whining about a football game."

Bradford stood up and walked around the desk. He leaned against it.

"Son, the football game is a big deal. Don't be sorry about it. Just go out there and throw your heart into it. Then if you screw up, well hell, at least you can say you tried. Okay?"

Chris stood up and reached tentatively to his father. His father leaned in, and their shoulders touched. Chris then turned to leave but stopped at the door. He looked back at his father. "Thanks, dad."

**Music: "Cat's in the Cradle" by Harry Chapin.
For Bradford and Chris**

Chapter 11

Week Two, Day Five

We do no great things,
only small things with great love.

--Mother Theresa

Allison headed out to the garden at nine a.m. Luis nodded to her as she headed over to the geraniums she was planting as ground cover to fill bare areas. She had never seen geraniums like these with small light green leaves and white flowers. She knelt down before the plants, running her hands through the leaves, then smelling the wonderful scent they released. My god, how nature gives back, she realized.

At four p.m. Kelley came directly home from school. She went straight to her room, pulled on a pair of jeans and an old sweatshirt and walked straight through the sunroom to the garden. She spotted her mother working along the left fence. She was standing beside a wheelbarrow, wiping her brow. Kelley had never seen her so involved in anything in her entire life.

"Okay," she called out as she walked over. "How can I help?"

Allison turned, grinning broadly. "How wonderful! You're going to help me again? I'm so glad. That slave driver Luis has been on my case all day long!" she said loudly.

A grunt came from gardener, who was finishing the sealing of the pond.

"So, what are we doing?" asked Kelley.

"Well, I got to give it to this guy. He's smart. Since many of the plants won't be big enough to fill their spaces, he had these beautiful redwood chips delivered today. Our job is to cover every surface with chips that's not planted."

Kelley looked across the yard. "Wow!"

"Oh, it's goes very fast. We just throw the stuff. Don't worry; it's light as a feather." She picked up a handful and tossed it at Kelley, hitting her in the chest with it.

"Mom!" yelled Kelley, shocked. She went straight for the wheelbarrow, grabbed a handful and threw it right back at her. Her mom saw it coming and stepped out of the way.

"Girl, you gotta' be pretty quick to catch your old mom!"

Kelley laughed and the two began spreading the chips with abandon.

By late afternoon they had covered most of the yard. Kelley rolled the wheelbarrow over to the pond, and they began spreading the remaining chips in that area. Luis was on his knees, checking the water lines.

"Luis," said Kelley. "I don't mean to complain, but this pond doesn't look that large. How many fish you gonna' put in here?"

Luis stood up, walked over to Kelley and turned to face the pond. "We will put four orange, white and brown spotted koi in here. I'll test the ph of the water tonight, and they are scheduled to be delivered in the morning. The men know where to put them."

"But, aren't koi big fish? I mean, will they fit?" asked Kelley, clearly concerned.

Luis smiled. "Kelley, did you ever read <u>The Phantom Tollbooth</u> by Norman Juster when you were a child?"

Kelley grinned. "Yea, that was a great book! The kid, Milo, drives through the magic tollbooth into the Kingdom of Wisdom."

"Well, then perhaps some of Mr. Juster's wisdom is appropriate here. I believe he said at one point 'From here that looks like a bucket of water, but from an ant's point of view, it's a vast ocean; from an elephant's point of view, just a cool drink; and to a fish, of course, it's home.'"

Allison put her arm around Kelley and gave her a hug. They both smiled. Then Kelley suddenly looked at her watch.

"Mom, I got to go!"

"Go? Where?"

"To Chris's game. I have to be there for him."

Allison looked concerned. "Kelley, you know your father has grounded you. Leaving will make him very angry."

"I know, mom, but Chris needs me. He's really nervous."

"Nervous? Why?" asked Allison.

"The first string quarterback got hurt, so there's a good chance Chris will play. Mom, Chris is not the self-confident kid he pretends to be. He's really scared."

"Oh my!" said Allison. "I had no idea. He always acts with such bravado."

"That's Chris, mom. But believe me. I need to be there." Kelley paused. "Mom, why don't you go too? I mean, dad can't give me such a hard time if you're with me."

"Oh, you don't fool me. You're just trying to get us both in trouble," she said grinning. "Plus I don't know a damn thing about football. And I need to stay here and finish the garden."

"I can easily finish this up, Mrs. Sparks," called Luis from the edge of the pond.

Kelley looked at her mother. "Mom, it would mean so much to Chris."

Allison looked at her daughter with a lump in her throat. She reached out and grabbed Kelley by the shoulders. "Well, why the hell not! Let's go!"

*　　*　　*　　*　　*

Bradford watched the Friday Wall Street sell off all afternoon. Once the Dow fell over four hundred points, he knew the crisis was not going away. At quarter to five he received an email to begin preparations to lay people off on Monday. Guiltily, he hunkered down at his desk until everyone left. He had been a regional manager for five years, during the boom times, and he had never fired anyone. He dreaded it, especially here in the fall. It would be very difficult for anyone to find a job before the New Year.

As the final employee left, he reached for the last bundle of subprime loan contracts to send in. Normally he kept a preaddressed envelope in his bottom drawer, but he couldn't find one. He rose and walked back to Juanita's desk, knowing she would have some. As he sat down in her seat, he realized she would be one of the first to go. "Last hired, first fired as they say in business," he mumbled aloud. He found the envelope and started to get up, but noticed Juanita's family pictures on her desk. Funny, he had never looked at these before, nor had he asked Juanita about her family. It appeared she had two teenage sons and a younger daughter. In a separate frame to the right was her wedding picture. As Bradford reached for it, he saw a small paperweight with something inscribed on it. He picked it up and read aloud. "We are prone to judge success by the index of our salaries or the size of our automobiles rather than the quality of our service and relationship to mankind. Dr. Martin Luther King, Jr."

Bradford set the paperweight down and walked back to his desk. I've got to get these contracts out, he thought. Suddenly the phone rang. He ignored it. As he shoved the contracts into the envelope, the answering machine picked up the message.

"Mr. Sparks? This is Mrs. Kowalski. I just wanted to thank you again for looking out for me. You know I watch the evening news every night, and it just looks terrible today. So, thank you again. Bye now."

Bradford froze. He stared at the contracts halfway inside the envelope. Mrs. Kowalski's was in there. She would lose everything. He started to search for hers, then stopped. "What am I doing?" he said aloud. "Everyone of these people will be screwed."

He sat silently for a moment, thinking, then stood up. Bradford dropped the entire stack into the garbage can and left.

*   *   *   *   *

Maria heard the gravel crunching under the wheels of the Cadillac Escalade. She continued chopping the garlic for the fish stew she was preparing, throwing in a small handful into the rich tomato-based sauce.

"Hey, Maria!" Bradford called out as he walked into the kitchen.

Surprised to be greeted, Maria turned around smiling. "Well, Mr. Sparks, nice to see you home."

"What's for dinner? Smells good. Jeez, I didn't realize how hungry I was."

"Well, my Catholic habits die slowly. It is Friday so I thought I would make a nice Spanish fish, shrimp and mussel stew. It needs to simmer but each of you can eat it when you're ready."

"Where's Allison?" asked Bradford as he reached for a boiled shrimp. Maria smacked his hand, hard.

"She has been working in the garden all day. Kelley came home and helped. Then they left."

"Left? Kelley? She left this house when she knew she was grounded?"

"Yes," said Maria, turning to look at Mr. Sparks. "She left with her mother. They have gone to see Chris play."

"Allison? Football?" Bradford said, snickering. "Oh come on, she just did that to make me angry."

Maria chose not to reply to this remark. She picked up the knife and began chopping an onion. Bradford looked away, out the kitchen window. Outside he saw the gardener digging in the dirt. "Oh, damn. It's Friday. I need to go pay him," he mumbled to himself.

Bradford walked back to his study and laid his briefcase on his desk. Over the last few years he had always loved this time on Fridays went he mentally went through the contracts sent out that week. He felt fulfilled, even exhilarated, as he saw the company profits and commissions growing. Tonight as he set the briefcase down his spirits fell, realizing how bad things had gotten. How would he pay for everything?

"Well, quit whining," he said to himself. He pulled out the file of unpaid bills, deciding to pay off the smaller bills he owed first. Reaching for his checkbook, he remembered he still hadn't paid the gardener. Damn, he thought. I might as well as get him out of here first.

Grabbing a calculator, he figured the days Luis had worked times the minimum wage, wrote a check, then walked through the house and out the sunroom door. He had only taken two steps outside when he stopped in his tracks. A backyard of flat prairie was now enveloped in layers of lush green, punctuated by light and shadow, adorned with spots of contrasting stone. It pulled you into its calm and quiet.

Bradford spotted the gardener in the middle of the yard on his knees by the stream. Luis turned when he heard the man approach.

"So, you about finished here?" Bradford said.

"Yes, sir. These are the last plants to go in. My final task is to make sure the lighting is working, and I am done."

Bradford looked over Luis's shoulder. "What is that you're planting? I've never seen a plant with green and brown leaves, red stems and yellow flowers."

"This is oxalis, sir."

Bradford's head jolted back, shocked. "What! Isn't that the crap I am paying you to pull out?"

Luis smiled. "Mr. Sparks, plants are like people. If you don't come to know them, it is easy to see them as all the same. This is a different species of oxalis. It doesn't spread."

"Oh," said Bradford, leaning over to inspect the plant more closely. "You do seem to know what you're doing out here. I have to hand it to you. This yard looks completely different."

Luis stood up. "Thank you, sir. I do love my work. But, I imagine you love your work also."

Bradford cocked his head sideways. "Why do you say that? You don't even know what I do."

"Well, sir. I see how much time you devote to your work. I imagine you either love it or you owe someone a lot of money," Luis said with a laugh.

Bradford kicked the dirt with his shoes. Luis could tell he had made the man uncomfortable.

"Well, sir, I don't want to keep you. I'm sure you want to hurry to your son's game."

Bradford looked startled. "Why do you think I'm going to his game?"

"Well, your wife and daughter left to see your son play. I assumed you would do the same."

Bradford chuckled. "No, my job is to stay here and make sure my wife and daughter can continue to spend my money."

Luis looked confused. "I don't mean to pry, sir, but you look big enough to have played high school football."

Bradford straightened up. "Damn straight. I was pretty good too. A defensive back. I loved knocking the hell out of a running back coming through the line."

Luis smiled. "I bet your father loved watching you too."

Bradford's expression immediately turned angry. "Look, my old man was a violent drunk. He never came to my games. I succeeded in spite of him."

Luis looked deeply into Bradford's eyes. "I'm so sorry, sir. That must have been so painful for you, growing up without seeing your father's love, having to struggle on your own. Chris is very lucky to have a father who supports him."

Bradford felt a sudden weight in his chest and a lump in his throat. He shoved his hands into his pockets and turned to walk away, then felt the check.

125

"Look, here's your check. Thanks for the great job."

Luis did not reach out to take it. "Excuse me, Mr. Sparks. Your wife has already paid me."

Bradford shoved the check back into his pocket. "Oh, she did, huh? If you don't mind me asking, what did she pay you?"

Luis smiled. "That sir, is between your wife and me."

Bradford chuckled and turned to walk away. The lights along the flagstone path suddenly came on automatically. The rose-colored stones glowed before him. He stopped and turned around. The entire garden shimmered. Reaching back into his pocket, he pulled out the check, handed it to Luis, then strode quickly towards the house.

*   *   *   *   *

By the fourth quarter Freeman led by three touchdowns. Playing Tucker High School had been the perfect first game without Chase. Tucker had won only two games the entire season. Their small front line was unable to stop Freeman's running game.

Coach Preston called Chris over with eight minutes left in the fourth quarter.

"Okay, Chris, you're going in. We don't want any heroics here. Just run the clock out. This is a great time to practice hand-offs. I'll send the plays in. Remember, whatever you do, *don't* run out of bounds and stop the clock and *don't* throw an interception. Okay, son?"

Chris nodded and Coach patted him on the back as he ran in with a group of freshman linemen. The first play was a run to the left. Chris called the play, stepped up and took the snap. He turned left and handed the ball to the left halfback. Two Tucker defensive linemen had broken through though and cut him off. The halfback turned and ran the other way. He was caught ten yards behind the scrimmage line. It was now second down and twenty.

Chris expected a pass to come in, but it was a run up the middle. They gained four yards back. He looked at the sideline and the clock. Five minutes left. It was third and sixteen. Tucker had no more time outs. Please, he thought. Let me throw one, just one. The play came in from the sidelines—a handoff to Taylor, the right halfback, for a run up the right side.

Chris dejectedly called the play, and the team broke for the line. He took the snap from center and spun to the right but there was no halfback! Taylor had run the wrong way. Chris pulled the ball in and kept running along the line looking for a hole, but he saw only a wall of Freeman and Tucker jerseys. No heroics, he remembered. Eat up the clock, he thought. As he scrambled, something caught his eye downfield. Someone in a blue Freeman jersey was waving frantically.

Chris stopped, planted his back foot, and threw the ball with all his might. He had just let it go when he was shoved across the sideline into the opposing team's bench. Two of the Tucker players made sure he went down hard. He lay waiting.

Downfield on the opposing team's thirty yard line, "Can't Catch It Carlson" had done what he had been taught. On a busted play, get free and get the quarterback's attention. Steve looked up and saw the ball coming. He realized that if he kept moving, he would outrun the pass, so he stopped and stood in the middle of the field. A Tucker defensive end saw the ball fly over his head. He followed it's trajectory to Steve and took off running. Steve watched the ball sail towards him, but he also saw a red jersey coming fast.

"Come on, ball. Come on, ball," he kept saying to himself. "Catch it and hold it, no matter what happens."

At the last second he realized he needed to move to the right to make the catch. He stepped and cupped his arms. The ball landed with a jolt and started to bounce away, but he closed his arms over it. He felt something brush his left leg. Looking down he saw a red jersey sailing past. That one step had saved him. He turned with one thought in mind. RUN!

Steve moved his skinny legs like they had never moved before. The yard lines became a blur. He could hear the crowd's roar getting louder. Off to his left a referee appeared, running with him. Steve locked his eyes on the black and white striped shirt and ran harder. Suddenly the ref stopped and raised both arms. The home crowd exploded. The band started up the fight song. Steve stopped, bent over, and gasped for breath, then straightened up and turned around. Ten yards away he saw most of the Freeman players running right at him.

"They'll crush me," he mumbled.

But they didn't crush him. Johnson and Diller got to him first. Each grabbed a leg and lifted him up, sitting him on their shoulders. As the other players arrived, they jumped up to slap Steve anywhere they could reach him. They carried Steve off the field back to the bench where Coach Preston reached up and plucked the thin boy off the players' shoulders and patted him on the helmet.

Chris had jumped up when he heard the crowd roar, but he couldn't see over the Tucker players.

"I can't believe it!" he yelled. "I missed another completion."

He pushed his way through to the sideline and stared downfield. His teammates were carrying some Freeman player around in the end zone.

"Oh my god!" he yelled and began jumping up and down. He started to run down to the end zone, but realized everyone was headed for the home bench. He ran across the field and fought his way into the center of the crowd of cheering players. There stood Steve Carlson, the boy whom the team had hazed so cruelly in the gym, grinning from ear to ear and hugging the football. Steve and Chris yelled when they spotted each other. They ran towards each other and jumped in the air, bumping shoulder pads like they do in the pros. The crowd in the stands roared.

Steve jerked his helmet off with one hand. Without hesitation he handed the football to Chris.

"Here, Chris. You threw it. You deserve it." Chris looked down at the ball. His heart told him what to do.

Chris handed Steve back the ball. "No, Steve. You caught it and ran it in. You made it happen."

Chris turned and jumped over the bench to look for Kelley in the stands. Then he remembered. She's grounded. She missed my touchdown, and it's my damn fault.

Dejected, he turned back to the bench, but suddenly heard a familiar voice calling his name. He whirled around and began searching frantically. Kelley always sat near the fifty-yard line. Finally he spotted her over to the right.

He waved frantically, jumping up and down. Kelley was screaming his name. She waved back, then pointed to her right and to her left. Chris stopped jumping, his arms dropped to his sides; his mouth fell open. Kelley was standing between his mom and dad, and his dad was cheering.

*   *   *   *   *

For the first time in years the family climbed into the Cadillac Escalade together. There was a big after-game party at someone's house, but Steve and Kelley were happy to be in the car with their parents. Bradford took everyone out for burgers and milk shakes. They relived the touchdown again and again at the table, laughing that Chris never got to see his biggest plays.

Finally they headed home. As Bradford pulled into the driveway, he stopped halfway down.

"Chris, you got your car keys?"

Chris looked confused. "Yes, sir."

"Well, how about you move your car over into my spot, and I'll take yours this weekend," he said, turning around and smiling at his son.

"Cool!" yelled Chris as he jumped out of the car.

Maria was standing in the open garage in amazement. "*Dios mio!*" she mumbled.

Chris moved his car and the family headed inside. Maria gave Chris a big hug. "I listened to the game on the radio, *mijo*. Bravo! Now, I've made a little party in the sunroom to celebrate. I will not take 'No' for an answer. Everyone. *Vamos!*"

The family traipsed back through the house laughing and talking, but as each entered the sunroom, they grew silent. Maria had lit only a few candles and had opened all the windows. They stood in silence, in disbelief at the beauty outside.

The garden was lit. Soft spotlights shown on each of the three waterfalls. Lights illuminated the arched

130

bridges. The Mondo grass around the patio shimmered. Shadows fell from the stone sculptures standing stoically in the white crushed quartz that had been raked into concentric circles. The winding flagstone pathway from the sunroom all the way to the patio was lit with short lights that wore small caps. And at the base of the old tree, Luis had placed two spots shinning upwards so that the tree's canopy reflected a soft glow back to earth. The only sound in the yard was the rustling water of the stream running over the waterfalls and into the pond.

Bradford turned to Allison. Her face was aglow. She looked at him and smiled.

"Oh my god," she exclaimed. "It's so beautiful! Luis said something about lighting, but I had no idea what effect it would have."

Kelley stepped through the sunroom door. "Mom, it's amazing. I can't believe it."

Chris followed her out. Bradford took Allison's hand and pulled her out the door too. Maria followed.

They walked along the flagstones, taking it all in. At the patio in front of the coach house, they huddled.

"Mom, where's Luis?" asked Kelley, concerned.

"He left a couple of hours ago when he was finished," answered Maria. "I saw him walking down the driveway with his satchel."

"But why?" asked Kelley.

Bradford hung his head. "I'm afraid that's my fault. I told him last week to leave when he was done."

Bradford looked at his wife. "Allison, I'm sorry. I will find him tomorrow."

"Dad!" exclaimed Kelley. "You have to! Tomorrow is the garden competition!"

Allison held up her hand. "No, no, he doesn't. I don't care what those people say about our garden tomorrow."

She turned to look at her children and husband, together.

"I've already won."

Music: "Rhymes and Reasons" by John Denver. For Luis and all Teachers

About the Author

Bill McBride drew on many of his own professional and personal experiences to write *Carrying a Load of Feathers*. In his years in education, he has taught Language Arts, Social Studies, Drama, Gifted and Talented, and Reading. He holds a Masters and a Ph.D. from the University of North Carolina at Chapel Hill.

Bill has also been a textbook author, editor, and national consultant for major publishing companies. Currently he works independently and is known internationally as an inspirational speaker and motivational teacher trainer.

Carrying a Load of Feathers is the second of a series of books involving Luis, the gardener. His first book in the series, *Entertaining an Elephant,* has now sold over 80,000 copies. Half the proceeds of both books go to the AIDS charity Under One Roof. For more information on Bill's workshops, visit his web site at www.entertaininganelephant.com.